Silent Riders of the Sea

For Fawn Aoife Fagan

"Somewhere you made a choice. All followed to this."

— Cormac McCarthy, *No Country for Old Men*

Silent Riders of the Sea

By

John Gerard Fagan

First published in paperback special edition, 2024
By Cybirdy Publishing
101 Camley Street, London N1C 4DU, UK

Published by Cybirdy Publishing
Cover page by John Gerard Fagan
Illustrations by John Gerard Fagan
Typeset by Simon and Sons ITES Services Pvt. Ltd
Printed by Hobbs the Printers Ltd

This book is typeset in minion, Proxima Nova and Copperplate.
A CIP record for this book is available from the British Library

ISBN: 978-1-0686782-9-5

Silent Riders
of the Sea

John Gerard Fagan

- 1 -

to the unknown

the dead of night on an Arctic ship
as close to hell as his imagination could construct
groaning metal and the lip vibrations of exhausted men
pale and unwashed figures
ice spreading on their dreamless faces
the ship was alive in the wee hours
beating cold blood inside colder flesh
Jack shivered in his bunk and blew into bruised palms
the soiled blanket took more warmth than it gave out
wiped a mop of dead yellow hair off his face
and tried to force himself to sleep once more
death was on board
and waiting with sharpened claws in bleached shadows
it would eat again before long
the gaffer was making a racket on deck
and monologuing to the pale sea again
drunk on their non existent supply of whisky no doubt
the taste of iron slushed down Jacks throat
he coughed up a palmful of something dark n sticky

and wiped it on his pillow

should have stayed in his wee town

stayed down the coal mines

stuck to what he knew

less pay

but a better chance of making it home alive

knew that now

too late

far too late

he curled up

and tried to ignore the sick mens screams

cold rot pouring out their hot gubs

been out almost a month at sea

still several more away from the nearest shore

they would all be silent by then.

- 2 -

the north awaits

they set out at dusk
sunk into the deep depths of winter
dark turned waters that descended beyond reason
the walls were breathing
smelled like industrial January
dreich
smoke n fear in the air below
on deck the wind was like a rusty blade
all beyond a hands reach dissolved in the fog
watery mouths dried with carpets of vomit
hours felt like months on board
Jack hadnt ever been on a ship before
never mind one that sailed past the furthest northern isles
deep into the white wastelands
fear touched him with soft fingers
from the moment the whistle sounded
and rope n anchor ripped from the shore at Aberdeen
and the ship sailed away from the creaking pier in voiceless silence
it felt wrong
it all felt wrong.

crushed cabins

his sleeping room was cramped and maukit
bunks littered with dusty horsehair blankets
that hadnt moved since the century before
twelve beds in the one he was assigned
his at the bottom
furthest from the door
and harboured the breath n stench of frightened men
like gas pumped into a cracked glass bottle
couldnt unravel
if he straightened his legs hed be right into the bunk of the next fella
putty n wood shavings soaking up leaks n spillage
historic mould of forgotten men in the shadows
kept his boots within a hands reach
a fair few had cracked cardboard soles and no laces
eyes on his miners ones were never far away.

a mouthful of wingless moths

a still October evening that threatened to rain
they had eaten dinner without as much as a smile exchanged
been the same for weeks before he was due to depart
sunlight faded from the window like a heinous dream
she broke the silence
whispering not to go on that ship
had a bad feeling burrowing through her gut
and they had to really talk
not just keep postponing
put her hand over his on the table
he swallowed
but his bag was packed and at the door
long since made his mind up
it was too late
already signed off from the pit
his old job was long gone
the chance of him dying down the mines
was higher than most jobs in Scotland
maybe them all

so this was a good move forward
a hollow thump echoed from his chest
he knew what she didnt
knew better
she worried for him down there
but she didnt have to with this new job
much safer
no roofs caving in with rocks like bullets
no cages firing him down at the speed of a freight train
this ship business was far far safer
treated like men too
too good an opportunity to turn down
only had to work six months a year at most
he would be back within four weeks after this first voyage
and every second month he would be home
it would help them move on
change their lives for the better
she was sleeping when he left before dawn
didnt even say goodbye.

- 5 -

seasick

his pillow was wet with piss that dripped from the bars above
a white haired man with rodent teeth mouthed an apology
to pay for the embarrassment
he offered a pair of brown woollen gloves
Jack refused n whispered it was no bother
turned the pillow over
was the least of his problems
most men were worn to a shadow with seasickness
and displayed the contents of their stomachs over chests n sleeves
bile half mopped swirling on the floor
sticking to skin
melted into the cold dark silence
kept his eyes on an orange light by the stairs
to stop the world from spinning
and spinning
and spinning.

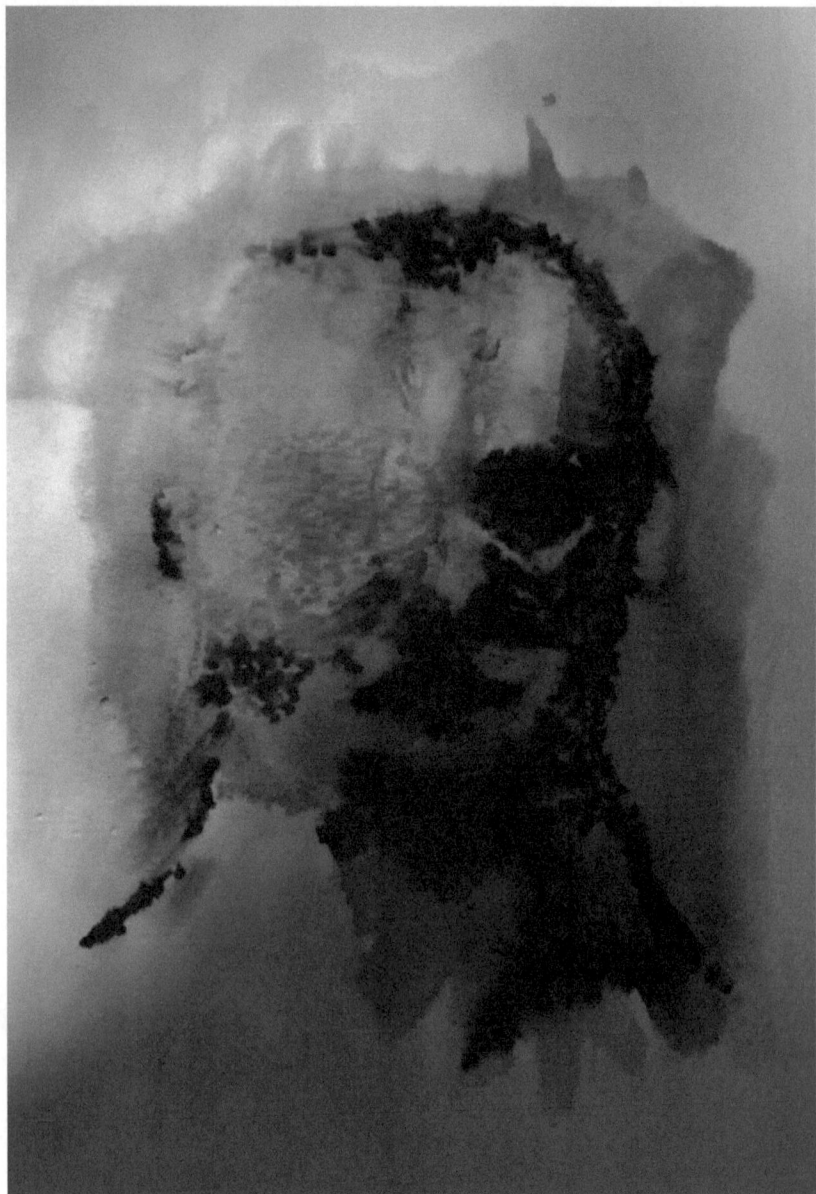

- 6 -

the new job

the first two days on board passed in thick silence
sailing over foaming waters
blue drift nets itching for a taste of the sea
night approached
candles dripped in their own greasy waters
men from all over Scotland
huddled together on deck for warmth like long lost animals
a half leaking sky was pregnant with storm
the gaffer had a glint in his eyes
his grip on that stock whip
and clenched teeth at the slightest infringement
showed beyond certainty he had a taste for mindless violence
he cleared his throat n spat

men
listen up
and listen good you fucking pieces of shite
tomorrow we will fill the belly of this ship
fill her to the brim with juicy fish

and can them before they sour
hundreds of thousands of cans to be filled to feed the nation
and we wont return until we do
you have all been assigned an important role
and shown your duties
so I dont want any grief
any moaning or complaining
in case you havent realised
this isnt the pit or a factory
where at the end of a shift
you can fuck off back home for a kiss off your mammy
this is my house you are living on
mine
you hear

mine
Im the gaffer
and while you are here
what I say goes
follow my orders n we will get this done nice n early
and be home in three months tops
I ken youse were told four weeks
but thats no use to me
no fucking use
lets be realistic eh
three months is what Im asking for
so give me all you can
and youse will all have much more money

we all will
money is what youre here for
so lets make some eh
the nineteen thirties are a time of prosperity for all men
and we are all here to take advantage of that
you are in the right place to make a tidy sum
exactly the right place
fucking lucky bastards if I dont say so myself
I am a Glasgow man born n bred
but I have not been back for years
and I would rather I didnt have to go back to that shithole
so this venture will be a success this time around
I ken it
we have got the right crew this time
so just to make sure this all sticks in your thick skulls
heres how things work
I get paid from the company
youse all get paid from me

Jack stopped listening
and nibbled at the skin around his thumb
nails bitten to stumps
couldnt remember when he picked that childhood habit back up
the gaffer waltzed in between them
strolling in an atmosphere that wasnt like theirs at all
as if he existed in an entirely other place of being
he was built close to the ground
face covered in squirming blue veins

17

voice getting louder
skin stinking of sour wine n strong onions
the waves like the wings of dragons were beating overboard
men flinched from the spray
half sleeping Jack floated inside himself
tried not to sink into the past
the present was hard enough
his fingers too numb to hold a cigarette
no chewing tobacco left
feet were blocks that stretched cracked skin
every part of him was shivering
cold enough to crack bones n freeze blood

now get a good fucking sleep men
by sunrise youll be dragging those nets out from the deep
and I am telling youse
you all better be fucking listening
cos I wont be repeating myself.

- 7 -

dawn

the noise set his teeth on fire
morning came with the sound of men ringing bells
like it was a wedding
pungent odours swirled throughout the roaring vessel
they poured out bunks
and on to the frost that lined the wooden floor
up damp stairs that were worn down like old bars of soap
breath bloody in their throats
soiled yellow light of the rising sun revealed all
a few familiar faces from the mines back home
most of those were fillers or cutters long past their prime
a tall one with a twisted arm from a gas explosion
at the colliery two towns over
and frequented his home town in the winter shifts
two men older than what his father would have been
both long past retirement but no doubt lost their pensions
one wee fella who was half blind with eye disease
the youngest were the blasters sons
two red headed brothers with nervous twitches

all none too bright
a smile grew on Jacks face
as if he was some genius n didnt see this coming
they all fell for the same snake oil pitch
unemployment rife
most too old or sandbagged to work down a pit anymore
and the best paying job in all of Scotland comes along
offers them a miracle
wives children grandchildren needing fed
the mines didnt need most of them in spring n summer
and not even them all in winter
the trawler work was an opportunity of a fucking lifetime
much much easier
even an invalid would coast it
would make them all rich
he shook the memories that flooded
and poured them on to the floor
shuffled in puffs of bruised breath on to the deck
and got hands into the first catch
cutgutcansealrepeat
cutgutcansealrepeat
cutgutcansealrepeat
some waste swept into buckets for their supper and bait
the rest off the sides into the iron blue water
cutgutcansealrepeat
cutgutcansealrepeat
cutgutcanseal repeat
cutgut canseal repeat

cutgut can seal repeat

cut gut can seal repeat

cut	gut	can	seal	repeat
cut		gut		can
seal		repeat		

repeat

repeat

repea

repe

rep

re

r

before morning ended

the adrenaline from the first shift of the new job had faded

gulls swarmed at their tail

their screaming song he felt beating in his chest bones

and trapped in a hollow ribcage

sitting n squatting too long without a stretch

felt like a blunt iron rod being pushed up the spine

coughs n runny noses

wet ash n smoke

plumes of mould in eye sockets

watering.

- 8 -

rats

he wiped condensation from the thick circular window
still couldnt see a thing out of it
greasy
fogged from the inside
permanently beaded with water
same as every other thing on the melting vessel
not even rats boarded that ship
those wee bastards had higher standards
and sensed its doom
no fat bluebottles in a dusty corner
a woodlouse or a centipede either
the company clearly thought the men working on it
were below those kind of beasties
well below
and treated as such as soon as they were away from the shore
cabins damp n diseased from the lack of sunlight
human faeces mixed with blood n vomit from the last voyage
left to harden in corners
dirt n mould blooming like weeds in summer

splintered wood soft to the touch
and crumbled in your fingers
those were the highlights of that ship
some rare men melted into the walls
but he glided off the wet surfaces
never settling into the new life
he sank into his bunk n waited for the dinner bell to ring
throat was closing over
mouth dry
hoped for something warm to drink
and anything slightly edible
nothing stirred for hours except the dignity of desperate men
when the bell did ring
the earlier clamour wasnt there
men already too weak n sore to move.

- 9 -

wasps in ears

so tired he could feel a heartbeat in his wrists n fingers
exhaustion was cement stuck in the throat
head feeling like it would float away from the inside
blood congealing to slush
when he tried to sink into sleep
it felt as if a wasp was thrashing around the back of his eyes
heard it coming for him over n over again
swatted mid black air
cracked his hand against the bed frame and winced
as if the work n conditions were not fucking hard enough
thumb n wrist throbbed in the wet darkness
bruises
sleeping on bruises
yellow flesh turning purple n black
a layer of dried salt foam coating every inch of skin
fatigue pushing shoulders
a great end to a long first week.

first death

three long days of fifteen hour shifts on deck
cries for more than a short piss break were silenced
when the gaffer swung his stock whip against raw faces
exhaustion swallowed them into the belly of the whale
fat slugs behind eyelids
inching forward but never moving
surrounded by water
and thirst was one of the biggest concerns
his fingers bled n wrists trembled
taste of iron forever in his throat
tongue swollen
the white haired man staggered to the side of the ship
mottled chest
teeth marks in translucent arm skin
eyes swimming in blood
orders for him to get back to work were squealed
he smiled
and threw himself overboard
screams n shouts n waves of panic to stop n get him out
but the ship kept on moving

the gaffer sucked his teeth n peered over the side

back to work men
we cant stop for a madman topping himself
there is always one on board
it pains me
it really does
but we cant stop
lets get back to work

any sign of the jumper was soon lost in the foam
cries of needing to turn back got louder
the gaffers face was reddening
back to work
whats that
no
no
I said no
we cant stop
trust me theres no saving a crazy bastard
what
no
I said no
what the fuck is so hard to understand
dont ask me again
there is always one on every voyage
it cant be helped
so wheesht
fucking wheesht
I said

the gaffer whipped n whipped the side of the ship
like a man possessed
until the men grew glue over their dripping gubs
and were silent

back to work
back to work I said
back to work
BACK TO WOOORK
and anyone else with the same idea as that loony
can just go right ahead
go right fucking ahead
nobodys getting paid
nobody if youse dont get right back to fucking work
right fucking now
fucking
fucking
useless
bastards youse
think youse can take advantage of my good nature eh
I will cancel all your fucking wages
this isnt a democracy
what I say goes
I fucking told youse this
I told youse over n over
and youse are still not listening
dont make me lose my temper
I am staying calm this time
now shut your mouths
do as I say
and get fucking back to those fucking fish.

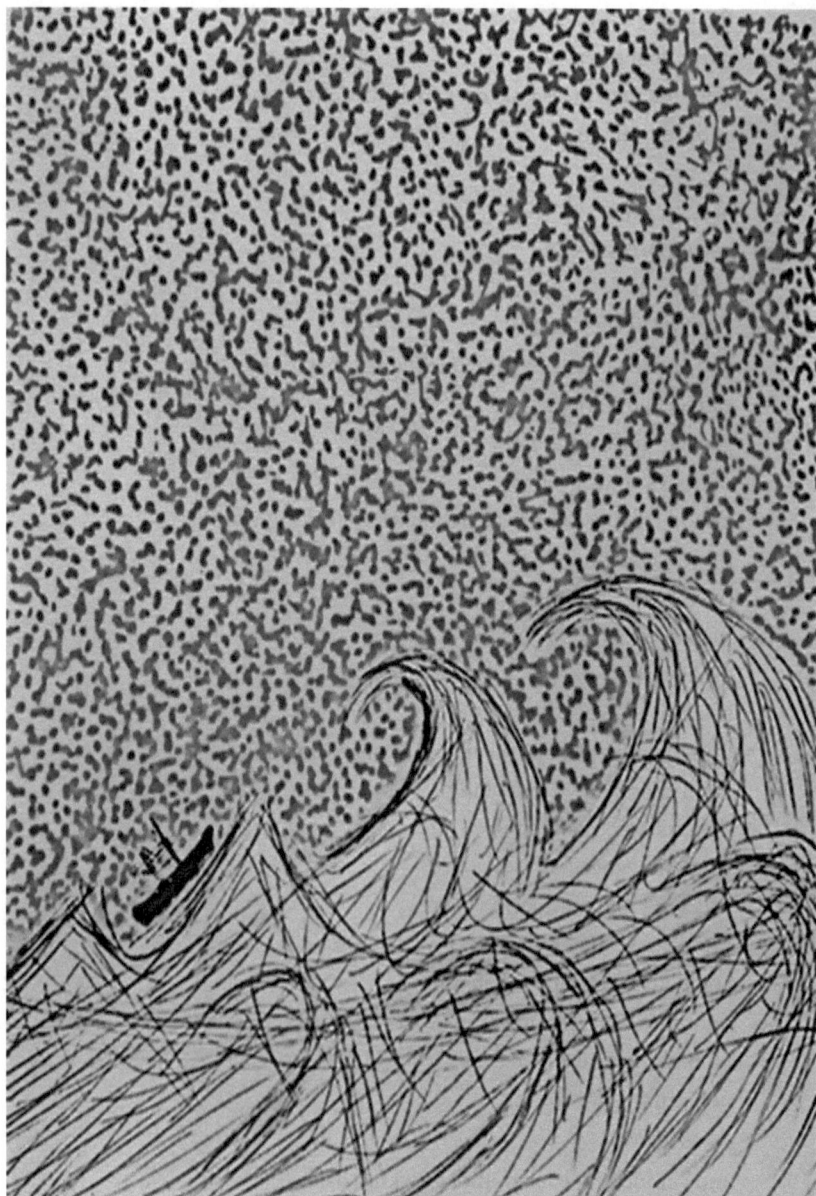

- 11 -

nowhere to turn

Jack lay in bed
unable to fade to the dark dreamworld once more
the bunk above empty
tried not to think of its last occupant sunk in that quilted blue ocean
breaking thin sheets as he fell
he was overtired
heart racing
would happen sometimes after a rough shift down the pits
mind just wouldnt switch off
the pains in his body played like an out of tune church organ
ulcers hatching on his gums
tongue swelling
cuts on hands pulsating
fingers like chewed prunes
pressed his eyes until he saw yellow circles behind eyelids
the wind sang with a deafening chime
and the ship bent to the left every ten heartbeats
could feel the waves lifting them up n up n falling down
belongings sliding across the floor

more n more eyes opened

as the sea swelled n the drops got deeper

higher

higher

higher

the drop ate his breath

and pulled the air out of him

water rushed all over the floor

higher

higher

higher

higher

higher

voices rose

was this it

this how he died

a wee ship being eaten alive by the great blue predator

the drop was accompanied by wails

like it was packed full of weans

fresh sour vomit sloshed on the floor with the seawater

he felt like he did when he was eleven

helpless

with nowhere to turn.

dark waves of winter

pale streaks of light
cans were all lined up coated in morning frost
and stuck together like melted chocolate
waiting on the first batch to spread across the deck
cold stillness
breath like chimney smoke from each man
he blew into his hands n stared into the void
calm clear waters
how vast those seas were
overwhelming didnt quite cover it
fear surfaced n stayed in his throat
the old ones using stars as maps
to navigate across all the madness
well beyond his understanding
he wasnt daft
but was a pit man
under the ground most of his life
and knew how to navigate that portion of the world
felt the same on the ship as the fish they dragged out

both in a place they didnt belong
out in the frozen furnace
hardly a man aboard not galloping towards the eternal rest
the first batch hit the deck with a sizzle
the gaffers men called out
he settled back into the monotonous rhythm
felt a terrible sadness for each fish
red tinged paste coated his mouth
face powdered from the dust of the dead
never felt more alone.

home was missing pieces

a door that stayed closed
the room it shielded like a shrine to a memory
of the last time their wee boy had slept there
the last night his wee face lay on that untouched pillow
Jack stood outside in the early days before going to bed
thinking that if he never opened the door
never even as much as peeked inside
that bed wouldnt be empty
he would be in there
in his wee blue n yellow jammies
just sleeping
under his wee blanket
it gave a slither of comfort
but nothing more.

- 14 -

selling dead milk

knowing what went into the tins
he was never eating any of it again
the smell alone was overpowering
as maukit as could be
wasnt even food fit for a housefly
when he got home
fish Fridays were going to be a thing of the past
would rather eat lumps of coal
that were pissed on by the mankiest of miners
never again
he wiped his nose with a wet sleeve
the sky rumbled and opened
the men didnt as much as flinch
until the cold twisted n soaked them
rainwater eroding the top metal layer of the ship
into a thin brown soup
feasting away at its bones
all at its mercy.

- 15 -

dusk

the drum of rain on the ship deck continued
burning water
acidic
consuming bone and beyond
black reeds reaching down from shivering thunderclouds
men worked wide eyed n trembling in the sizzle
water pouring down foreheads
hands wrinkled
cans rattled n hissed in the wind
fish flapped in the puddles on deck
distant n not too distant roars
blackened bones
white fins poking out torn jackets
the waves swelled
and carpeted the wooden boards
washing over boots
seconds like hours
and hours
and hours.

- 16 -

anything but fish

the scent of spoiled landflesh bubbling in pots
soaking in fat n salt
cracked cups n bowls they shared like pigs
the promise of decent scran
mashed potatoes soaked in butter
black pudding
scrambled eggs
scones
rice pudding for a dessert
never came to fruition
and a quick peek into the kitchen told him it never would
tea weak n watery
lukewarm porridge
rotten fruit
stale bread seasoned with circles of green n black mould
rot painted in blooms on the ceiling
little conversation leaked out from the men
thawing empty bellies n nursing sore gums
Jack was crabbit beyond belief

clothes n skin wringing
cough getting worse
chest rattling frozen peas
only a cold
only a wee cold
the gaffer passed around bottles of the cheapest whisky
like a demonic St Nicholas
there was plenty more where that came from
plenty
and if they kept up their efforts for three more days
just three
and take them past a fortnight at sea
they would get a half day off as reward
a day to take in the sights
and swirl some sweet brandy too if they fancied
or even sleep the morning away
it was their choice
he made a toast to their hard work
and to the life of the old yin
left to drift in those unforgiving waters
Jacks beard was growing wild n itched
envied those who set up their beds in the engine room
too warm sometimes they said
but none of them willing to swap even for an hour.

- 17 -

what lies within

sorrow was a frozen knife

cutting its way through white winter butter

took a while to fully get there

but by the end it was warm

so warm

and the butter was dripping off its side

and it kept on cutting

cutting

had a taste for it

storing heat n turning dark red

and turned to cutting through a ship in the Arctic

cutting through damp wood n rust

cutting through the deck to his cramped bunk

and took a rest in his gut as he stared

waiting to sleep

trying not to let it consume him

as it coiled like a wounded snake with few breaths remaining

and ate from the inside out.

- 18 -

hunger

the three days past
but the gaffer batted away any talk of the half days rest
said they were behind as it was
maybe in another few days they would be able to
Jack went to sleep that night full of anger
and woke feeling worse
everything was so much harder to do in the freezing cold
especially getting out of bed
no breakfast left by the time he got up
not even a mouldy piece of bread
just the fish n silent men for company on deck
stomach knotting
could have done with even a lick of sun juice in his stomach
swallowed the cold air
and shuffled into line
never thought so much about food in all his life
starving men worked harder was the gaffers thinking
even if it killed them.

- 19 -

wildlife

a seal got caught in the main net
and was tossed out with the fish on deck
it froze as all eyes flashed on it
the pale sun was drowning
didnt look as big as the pictures hed seen on the Aberdeen docks
a wean sized one at most
Jack stared
never seen such a strange thing up close
its big eyes bulged
nose twitched like a rabbit
sensed the fear in it
the gaffer creaked out his warm office swinging a club
and before anyone could draw a breath
he smashed it over the head
again
and again
and again
he spat n wiped sweat dripping from his grey eyebrows
booted the carcass back into the water

the gaffer n the nearest men to him were all freckled with blood

disgusting things
Ive seen what they can do
theyll not be getting any of my fish again
and it better not have torn my fucking net
keep your eyes peeled
and watch out for them
they are fucking thieves
and given half a chance
would eat every one of our catches
away
you hear me beasts
away
away.

- 20 -

blackberries

heading for dinner in the pitch black

had a craving for blackberries

in long lost summers

at the end of July

Jacks father used to take him n his sisters down to the glen

and look for bramble bushes

they would fill metal buckets for his maw to make jam

laughing n singing daft wee songs

soft leaves n grass

limegreen plants wet along the burn

nothing sweeter than those big berries

that almost burst at the slightest touch

all coming home with purple lips n fingers

back on the ship

cold potatoes n oily cabbage didnt quite hit the spot

but would have licked the pot clean

first thing he had eaten all day.

- 21 -

relentless

it rained again

and again

and again

the seas leathery grasp trying to make them one with it

fill them till they sank

waves rose

they were all feart

the miners that pretended that they werent

were

could see it in their eyes

all feart n with good reason to be

the old seamen

who no doubt had seen the water spin from all angles

a hundred times or more

looked like they wanted to be anywhere else

anywhere but on that ship

eyes sank to clenched hands

and to whispering words from the old book

fear so thick it had a warm n sour taste

yet still they plundered out deeper still

the gaffer with only one thing on his mind

breath smoking through the cold

the nets were cast once more

water swept back to the deep

fish were slaughtered

gutted

canned

floating on swollen waters

and all on board acted like they were not inches from death.

- 22 -

a song that no one sings

couldnt drift off right away
nothing unusual
limbs jerking
snoring mixed with rasping chests
he got up for a sip of rainwater n a painful piss
whitehot moonlight ate exposed skin on his face
as shooting stars filled the night sky
a few lost men on deck stared in silence
whisky shivers in his spine
no gap between the sea n black sky
stealing life from beneath
was talk from some fellas to ask the gaffer to let them go
pay them for the days they worked
and drop them off somewhere
the nearest port would do
willing to even take half of what they were due just to get off
but they were too far out to sea
long past the point of return.

birth

having a wean
it changes you
the man he was vanished the day that boy was born
vanished
the moment he held him
saw his greeting wee face
all wrinkled n coated in milky wax
a helpless wee laddie
they were all he had
couldnt imagine for a second abandoning that wee thing
like his maw did to him
would have been impossible
he would have rather died
on the day he was born
his son became the most important thing that ever existed
only lived to see him safe n happy
and make her proud
the three of them
their wee family
his everything.

- **24** -

bruised sky

the tins filled and kept on filling
face burning with the wind
he stared into the icy water
foam trailing from the sides like single cream
hadnt eaten nearly enough again
and felt that familiar hunger pain ferment
hadnt enough clothes on to be out in weather like that either
all would be provided for said the gaffer back in Aberdeen
the ship had the best of uniforms to battle the elements
the very best
but an old fishermans coat ripped at the left side
was far from what was needed
and he was one of the lucky ones
the harder you work the warmer youse will be
the harder you work the warmer youse will be
the harder you work the warmer youse will be
the mantra sung by those that didnt work at all
pure lies
he swallowed
as thoughts drifted to an unfocused image of her face.

- 25 -

erin

met at six when her family moved from Carntyne

married at nineteen

almost eight years to the day he left

seven of which were a warm summer afternoon

the last cold

grey

her dark red hair

skin covered in freckles

never as much as looked at another woman

never wanted to

she had the kind of beauty that went beyond poor clothes

nobody within a hundred miles could match her face

smile

kindness

never once complained

or asked for things others took for granted

she was worth ten of him

lost sight of that

now all he was

was lost

wanted to come back to her the man he used to be

before the tide was against them

still had that love

carried that fire

it was there under the clouds of smoke

didnt know if she felt the same

afraid to know

could only hope what they had didnt extinguish when he left

knew she was as broken as he was

suffering had left a coarse imprint on her face

he did nothing to help

should have been stronger

tears ran and hung on the corners of his mouth

a cut from a can brought focus back to the new water world

the blood swelled

and dripped

dripped

dripped.

- **26** -

shipwrecks

a rare break in production
he hobbled to the side of the ship n rested with the others
watched the calm waters through the engine smoke
catching a few lines of sunshine on his body
felt the pain in his lower back pulsate n threaten to evaporate
but not quite leave
waited for the next batch to pour with eyes sunk to the deep
the water was like glass
floating on a naked sea
what swam in the shadows below
could see tiny fish darting
fragments of bluish ice floating like ancient unseen creatures
darker shapes further down
how many shipwrecks were beneath them
festering in the underworld
the sailors amongst them talked as if it was in the thousands
Jack picked at a scab behind his ear
and his fingers came back coated in red
the water was calling to him

whispering that he should find out its secrets
felt lightheaded
needed a drink but none was to be had until dinner
a whistle blew
men swept seawater over and lined up the next cans
reds n greys n greens going overboard
murking the once clear water

what are you doing lad
one of the gaffers men nudged him with the end of a club
the fish are coming in
so get back in your fucking place before I break your jaw
do you not want to get back home
I sure as hell do
the faster we do this
and get all these filled n sealed
the sooner we all get the fuck off this thing
you hear me lad
miners
you are the fucking worst creatures
coal rats
he limped back to his wet slot on the floor
and back to the shadows
just stay where you are
and fucking work.

- 27 -

time

everything eases with time
thats what he got told when his father died
but some things cant
some hurts are too deep
always raw scar tissue
forever bleeding
sits under your eyes
at the top of your chest
and going forward that doesnt change at all
his father was a faded memory of faded moments
as was his maw
but his son
that was pain that kept on folding over
and twisting
and tightening
the first few weeks he was going to work sobbing
in the depths of loneliness
and even now
almost two years later
felt the same
the exact same.

thirteen days

ears were one of the worst things to have on an Arctic ship
swollen skin peeling
needles in n out
out n in
constant pain
like a searing hot poker against the scalp
the cold ate even through hats
hatless men were for the bing weeks ago
blackened n purple ears peeled off in the cabin
fell off with less than a scratch
grown men greeting like weans
trembling in their beds
rusted metal woven into rusted metal
clothes were being stolen from bunks
dead mens hats had new owners in minutes
the sickest ones preyed on by freezing eyes
and freezing fingers.

grey walls breathe

coal dust

never leaves fingernails

the skin behind knees n elbows

or ankles

peel skin back

and it would already be there in the new layer

marinated for fifteen long years

that all blended into one dark dream

many of the men he didnt know on the ship were miners too

could tell from their hands

eyelids

teeth

blue veined scars on their noses n foreheads

permanent markings

the older ones hunched from digging in the black bowels

the fishermen n factory types werent built the same

fatter faces

soft legs

years under the ground twists men into solid creatures

each day claiming more life than one on the surface.

- 30 -

dregs

the shift ended early
as the nets tangled n corks needed replaced
men darent not look like they werent busy
cans were all sealed packed n stored
deck swept n swept
the gaffer spat n waved them away out of his sight
men drank n sang n ate
basins of hot water to wash faces n thaw feet
even some coal tar soap
he felt life breathing back under his skin
limbs twitching back to life
smiles broke for the first time since they had left land
strength rising
felt he would make it
and the worst of it was over
heard the gaffer stumble out from his office
and march down the stairs
but not even he could ruin the

leathered an old yin who spilled a drink over his boots

and screamed

silenced the songs

there wasnt time for a party just yet

this was about money

his money

needed them to focus on fishing

useless pieces of shite

the dregs of Scotland

his men confiscated what remained of the whisky

said he would give it back once the days work was done

there was still work to be done

always work to be done

and they were blind if they couldnt see that

fucking blind

he eyed each man in turn for one sour look

itching for a fight

but none came his way

Jack slipped away to his bunk

and sank into a dreamless sleep.

- 31 -

where the sun beats

the seabirds that squawked n chirped
feeding off their discarded catch
were gone
didnt know how long that had been
just expected to hear their cries that morning
but all was silent
the skies were empty
not even a cloud for company
thin lines of sunshine on the water
waves hissing
so far gone from the world he once knew
a nervous energy sank into the bones in his chest
and a fresh loneliness hatched once more.

the land of his fathers

father
a shipbuilder on the Clyde
moved a few miles to the northeast
where pit work boomed in the outskirt shires
a better life than in the Glasgow slums
with its tenements thick with poverty
crumbling
men scrambling for any kind of work
the village sat in what used to be a big glen
with burns
bogs
peatland
fern n woods
and fields upon fields of cows n sheep n horses
a farmers old land distorted for a new era
belching chimneys
black bing waste heaps
high against the green Campsie hills in the background
but in the heart of the glen n woods

the signs of industry vanished

a walled garden

his father helped build the worker houses

in what became known as Timber Town

and raised his family there

as a child Jack ran in the fields of summer with his sisters

wet earth in the rain

soil under fingernails

tree swings

but the world changed

moved on

the great war

men were sent to France n never returned

not enough work for the men that came after

locals left n spread across the world like hot butter on toast

tickets poured out for years

to America

New Zealand

Canada

Australia

Jack was offered several opportunities after his marriage

but said no to them all

Glasgow didnt appeal

and was suffering worse ills than the mining towns

the labyrinthine slums of the big southern cities

wasnt a good option either

he didnt want to leave all his father had built for him

they would somehow make it work

somehow make the dwindling pit wages last

Scotland was home

more so their wee mining town

best place for their boy to grow up

not some slum

or foreign land thousands of miles into the unknown.

squall

all night he listened to the rain

soft decay of the ship seeping through crevices

liver coloured nails

knuckles pink n peeling

floating on water

listening to more n more pour out the invisible sky

never ending

needed to piss but the cold held him under the bedsheets

move n he would never get a slither of warmth back

sweating n stinking cold steam from inside a colder blanket

trapped in roaring darkness

breathless n blue

a crack running down his face

jaw separating from cheek

a pounding in soft tissue squeezing his stomach

fall asleep n the pain will pass

fall asleep n the pain will pass

fall asleep n the pain will

fall asleep n the pain

fall asleep n the

fall asleep n

fall asleep

fall

he swung his legs over the side

and pissed on the floor

letting out a silent gasp

the sound masked by the rain n sawdust

mixing with the blood already sleeping there

felt the pain in his kidneys lift as he crawled back under

pulled the blanket over his face

the drumbeat of the downpour went on

and on

and on

long past dawn and into the next evening.

- 34 -

cans n fish

drifting across the utter remoteness of the ocean
cold wind feeding on the skin around his nostrils
intolerable pain
Jack covered his face with a salty hand
the whole world dissolved into cans n fish
nothing more nothing less
he tried to find some kind of meaning to it all
something to keep going
how what they were doing was important
essential to Scotland
feeding starving weans
filling them with strength
but couldnt find it
it was all going to other countries hed heard
down south n on from there
the only Scots benefiting were the rich company owners
a sprawling sickness that was eating the world
not even the gaffer was getting that much out of it
the local rich working the local poor to death
to feed the foreign poor n line the pockets of the foreign rich
there was the only meaning he found.

- 35 -

scratching

no light save a half beating lamp by the door
a silent breeze whipped the skin off the dead n living alike
men huddled into the foetal position under blankets
and prayed
teeth of ice with the taste of salt
he picked a scab from his elbow
and rolled over to his other hip
bruises eating into bone
the cries of the sick itching
a moustached man with a salt tang to his voice poked his head out
he was two bunks along n held a dripping candle
hair like smoke and parted in the middle
smelt of earwax
and had a haunted look of a rabbit

here mate
dont scratch it like say
dont scratch
I ken them lice crawl into open bed sores so they do

and once they are in
they dont leave you like say
they shite their eggs into you
only crawl out you when you are dead like say
dont scratch if you can help it
I ken all about lice eh

his skin was raw n silver
arms n neck reddened by the cold n fingernails

I wont
cheers for your advice

no bother
hear mind what I said
just mind it eh
cos once that deed is done you cant go back
you just cant

he blew the candle out n floated back to his bunk
saw him most days until his demise
always with a look to remind him to follow his advice.

- 36 -

novel

light from a lamp filled the cabin
filling them all with darkness
the air a swollen cage of the sleepers breath
a whistle sounded
time to get back to work
the gaffer was marching around
waving an oiled stick about like an out of sync conductor
Jack was up and in the line to eat breakfast
before there was none of it left
thick dust in the corners
pieces of the men who went before them
etched into the fibres of the ship
parts nobody really sees or can ever claim back
thoughts swam as he waited
for a man that liked to read
when exhaustion didnt smash his skull in
he wished he had something to occupy his mind
instead of draining thoughts

or broken conversations about the past
he had left a Russian novel back in Aberdeen
could have done with reading it again

your worst sin is that you have destroyed
and betrayed yourself for nothing

a lot to learn from that Raskolnikov fella
Jack had never left Scotland
but had been all over the world through stories
Spain with Don Quixote
France n the Mediterranean with Dantes
even the Congo with Marlow
it showed plenty that the gaffer didnt have any on board
not even one novel
palms n shelves filled with only the dust of the dead.

- 37 -

swollen hands

an old fella working next to him had swollen hands n fingers
and could hardly fill the cans
arms thin as wires
he passed him every second can
just so it looked like the old yin could still work
the dark eyed fella across from them did the same
cut gut can seal
cut gut can seal pass
cut gut can seal
cut gut can seal pass
they kept the rhythm going until almost midday
the gaffer had noticed n watched with clenched teeth
he swung over and booted the old yins jaw
this wasnt a job that could carry men
invalids werent welcome
that was made clear
made crystal fucking clear
the old fella pleaded for another job
he could sweep

haul in the nets
scrub floors
even help the cook
he couldnt help that his hands were swollen
couldnt help it
he could fuck off was the reply
he was a canner and nothing else
his contract was to can
if he didnt can he wouldnt get paid a single shilling
there were more than enough invalids for the easy work
the stock whip was unleashed
and the old yin sobbed n screamed
piss darkened his trousers
Jack grabbed the gaffers arm without another thought
as another blow was about to rain down
told him to leave it out with a breaking voice
it was too much
he was old n just needed
three solid blows to the face stopped his words

dont you ever fucking touch me boy
and that goes for all of you disgusting cretins
this is my ship
my rules
how hard is that to fucking understand
why do I have to keep repeating myself
eh
worst fucking crew I have ever had

the fucking worst to ever darken this great ship
fucking miners eh
never again
never ever ever again is a miner getting on my ship

Jack lost a weeks wages
and put on a final warning
but old swollen hands was spared another blow
and given some hot water to dip his paws into.

- 38 -

shadow

woke up to a weight on the edge of the bunk
it pulled his blanket from his neck
couldnt see who in the predawn dark
but that familiar sour scent gave away who it was
Jack closed his eyes
and froze
could hear the gaffers yellow breathing
clearing his throat
clicking his tongue
basking in the dark
he left without speaking
at dawn his boots were missing
and he saw who had them on not long after
a flapping cardboard soled pair a size too small in their place
a foul stench rose from his new boots
he weighed up the options and sighed.

- 39 -

new arrival

she picked the name the day after he was born
after his father
what a beautiful wee boy he was
couldnt stop looking at him n smiling
in those first weeks
Jack woke long before the sun rose
cradling him before funnelling down the mines
keeping that image with him as he descended in the cage
and shuffled in the darkness to get to the coal face
his eyes his eyes
his nose her nose
crawling miles upon miles underground with calloused hands
made worthwhile
to see his wee face smiling when he got home
there was nothing better
tried to picture that first summer
rain on a warm pavement
and fold himself back into that shape
but the memory came forth as an oily dream
out of focus
lost.

- 40 -

eyes

cold grease coated noses n chins
windows behind smeared with handprints of dried blood
the routine took hold once more
and all worked in raw silence
the dark eyed fella had taken to sooking out the fish eyes
tasted delicious he said
like wee boiled eggs
word spread in voiceless whispers
and men copied
ravenous n half a day away from dinner
tasted more like eating wet glass
but he ate the odd one
before tossing the scraps for the pickers
if it kept him alive
he would eat the skin and the bones too.

a pod of killer whales

the sun lay in its last breaths
men flocked to the side of the ship
even the gaffer didnt halt the impromptu break
all stood in awe as they breached once more
and called out to the sky
stared with drained eyes
old swollen hands stood beside him
mouth open
lungs rattling with phlegm
nose running with pus n dripping over his lips n chin
a piece of sodden cardboard under his arm

magnificent beasts he said
and waved at the deep waters
magnificent.

- 42 -

black gold

airless heat
baked in your nose
the taste crunching in teeth
this was the bowels of the land
ribs of the earth
not built for eyes
thick with dust that clung to your throat
iron monsters roaring
cramped darkness
that required full concentration to navigate
simmering skin at every turn
ears pinned to the wooden props
for any sound of a falling roof
any unusual creek
toxic gas
fire was your enemy
if you got caught with matches or a lighter in your snap can
you would lose a full days wage
but she did exactly that by mistake
they were awake most of the night
with the wean having nightmares

and not thinking straight when it was time to get up n ready
she tucked matches n cigarettes beside his pieces n cold tea
and he marched to work
sent home at the mouth n docked
a rare day of light in winter
they took wee Jackie to the woods n built a den
slept huddled together by the living room fire
best day of the year
one of the best in his life
worth every lost shilling
the pit paid the bills
kept them fed n watered
but was an unforgiving place
men getting arms or legs crushed wasnt common in his mine
but wasnt rare
however
there were no bitter Arctic winds down the pit
no rain dropping like frozen needles
fingertips black with dust aye
but no frostbite
your body fell apart in both
but the thirst for heat n shelter from the cold
overruled any other
he would have given just about anything
anything for a warm flame in that early evening moment
anything
traded those with black lung n deafness n failing eyes
knew where he was on a river of coal
and how to tackle it
a cannery in cold beyond cold was beyond surviving.

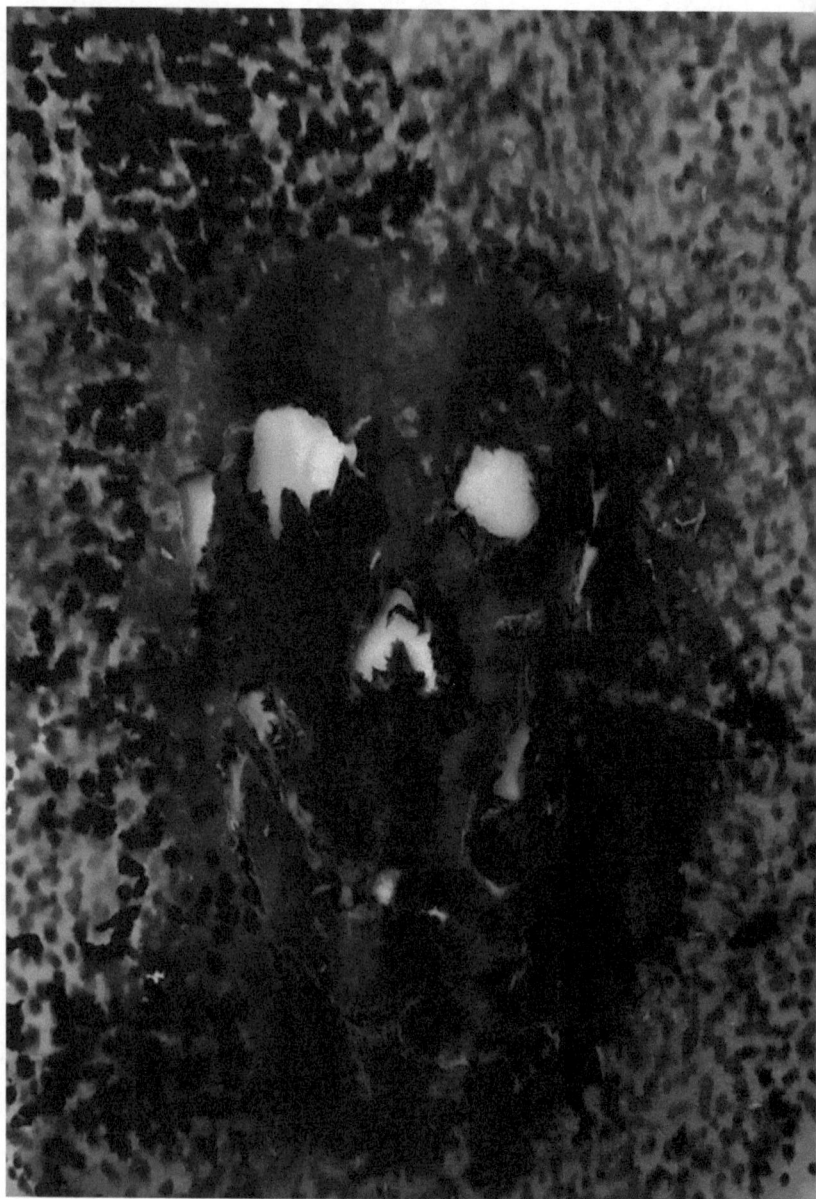

- 43 -

into the pale blue

as the men ate breakfast n sipped tea
the body of a young fella was hooked out of the water
screams n calls for help from the netters
was still alive
shivering n blue lipped
everyone rushed as one
blankets whipped off beds n swaddled
can he still work was the gaffers only concern
they left him in an empty bunk
a cup of hot tea would only be wasted on him the gaffer said
nobody comes back from that condition
but he gave in
and his men left half a cup by his head
as the rest were ordered to deal with the first catch
old swollen hands stayed beside him
by the time they got back down for supper
the bed was empty
the boys damp blankets already on several others
swollen hands staring into space
forsaken.

- 44 -

waves

relaxing
as a wee boy his father told him
that listening to the waves at night was relaxing
lived on the side of the River Clyde
and missed it every night when he moved to the shire
a soothing sound
a rhythmic crashing on the shore
fancy folk paid big money to live near the seaside
and hear the oceans song at night as they slept in warm beds
when she was a wee lassie
his maw stayed a few nights in Burntisland
and confirmed it was magical
but hearing the waves slap the sides of the ship
he felt nothing but fear
spiders of panic
would rather be alone in the glen at midnight
with the giant trees n flapping black birds
or in winter graveyards with the wildest of winds
than near the ocean n its piercing noise ever again
maggoty mutton for dinner rolled in his belly with each tilt

he leaned and spat into an overflowing bucket

swayed towards his bunk

palming for anything to steady his balance

the rise n fall

rise n fall

her breathing beside him at home was calming

but on the ocean the wind n waves were like breaths of fire

burning

brittle blue

he was a square sausage in a pan of lard

as the throat of the ocean waited

readying to swallow the limbs n cracked cartilage

of the broken men on board.

- 45 -

nemo

mining leaves men a long time with just their thoughts
a long time
got told when he first started to try and not think
to turn his mind off
and if he did the shift would fly by
tune out wee man just tune out
had to or it would be torture
nothing dragged like a shift down the pit
but his wasnt a mind to go off like a switch
instead he would rerun the stories from the novels he read
when he was a boy it was Moonfleet n Treasure Island
and as he got older the novels got bigger
and lasted a lot longer down there
a book like Waverley lasted a week
on the ship he tried to get lost in the world of Captain Nemo
but it was too painful to even think
took all his energy to try n stay warm enough to work
every second his mind was canning fish
feeling every sear of the wind
no cosy Nautilus
no escape.

- 46 -

incentives

production was low
far too fucking low
when they got back to Aberdeen
the gaffer was going to order the ripest whore for the man who
could fill the most cans
and make him proud
the offer didnt motivate as he wanted it to
so out came the tried n tested stock whip once more
hands n knees coated in wet salt that nipped cuts
the last thing any of them were thinking about
were whores in Aberdeen
especially ones of the gaffers taste
the sailors on board knew stories about him
famous in Lerwick for having his fill
with the roughest and oldest he could find
real women he said
real women
tried to even marry an old yin that had retired
and was consigned to the poorhouse
but she wouldnt go anywhere near him without being paid
and turned down his offer.

shame

instead of getting the messages before going home
like he promised
after a hard weeks work down the pit
he poured into the social club
just one or two quick drinks then he would buy their tea
plenty of time for a couple
wash the day away
clear his throat
that was all
what was the harm in that
he had earned it
but soon it was four five six
soaking his lungs in the cold warmth
and on to the races after to double their money
drank to take the taste of dust away
feeling with his tongue for bits of chipped bone n gristle
that were wedged into the space between teeth n gums
the drink kept flowing
and flowing

won the first race and felt invincible
but didnt win a single one after
lost a shoe and a full weeks wages by the end
every shilling
stumbled home
with the worst kind of sickness beating in his chest
wee Jackie sitting by the table waiting on his tea
was as sobering as any sight
but she never gave him a hard time over it
Erin went out
and borrowed vegetables n porridge from the neighbours
he wallowed in shame all through the following weeks months
shame that scalded worse than boiling water from the kettle
never gambled again
even just the thought of it
turned his stomach to the tightest of knots.

- 48 -

no longer human

as the days passed
old swollen hands looked less n less human
his eyelashes had frozen
eyebrows all iced over too
felt his own must have been the same
hair felt glued to his scalp
hardly an hour into their shift
felt like a Monday
but had lost count of the days
asked the dark eyed fella
and received a shrug as a reply
the wind picked up
sending refreshing saltwater into their faces
tried again to picture what it would have been like
relaxing in the Nautilus
sinking into a chair in the library there
wandering over to the dining room
but no clear image came to mind
the doors to that submarine were closed
was going to be a long day.

– 49 –

long lost summers

I miss jaggy nettles stinging my shins n ankles
rubbing docking leaves to heal them
bees on buttercups
putting itchy coos down your pals back n running away
picking thorns off rose bushes
dandelions in your mouth
rain in burnt fields
and sliding in that thick mud in gardens after a heavy shower
climbing bing heaps
and ruining the arse out of school trousers by sliding down them
feeding horses long grass from your palm
ladybirds landing on arms
catching tadpoles in the burn
hell even clouds of midges
I miss all of those summer days
the days before being sent down the mines
the days when my father was alive
and my maw was singing
as a grown man I miss them

the things I have taken for granted in life

and now its all gone

never coming back

and when I should have held on to wee Jackies summers

and enjoyed every second of him and my wife

I didnt that often

always thinking about the future

thinking there was always time later

later when I wasnt so tired

later when he was a bit bigger to take swimming in the loch

later

there was going to be so much more time later

so many more summers

but later was winter

alone in the Arctic waters

thinking about jaggy nettles.

- 50 -

overtime

the stench of the fish innards never left their skin
fingertips n palms reeking
when the gaffer allowed small pockets of sleep
it was all they could taste
smell
see
the blood of the fish mixed with his own
can lids were metallic teeth
took him too long to work out the safest way
but no way allowed for no cuts
shredded hands with no time to heal
on their knees just like in the pit
mining for fish
served the same purpose
one kept folks houses warm
the other their bellies
both wore the worker down to bones n beyond
the men swayed like broken waves on an unforgiving shore
one hour of overtime turned into two

three
four

enough complaining
I dont want to hear another fucking word
youse can rest when we are done
trust me your dinner will stay warm
cant waste a catch like this
nobody should be neglecting on their duties
the ship falls apart if but one of us does
but one
come on you shower of gits
move it
MOVE IT
the gaffers men seen to it all voices of concern were silenced
and hands kept moving one way or another
bastards the lot of them
who were hardly ever without salted meat in their mouths
puffing up
bellies warm under proper layers n waterproofs
and dipping into the gaffers office for a heat all the time
while the workers bodies were like wet paper
ripping apart
getting weaker by the hour

air so cold it cooked skin n flesh from bone
yet still they worked on
and on
and on
metallic dust floated in the lamp light
skin felt like rusted iron
when he finally crawled into his bunk
the room spun out of his throat
and it was light again before his muscles stopped twitching
and they were marched back on deck to dance once more
condemned.

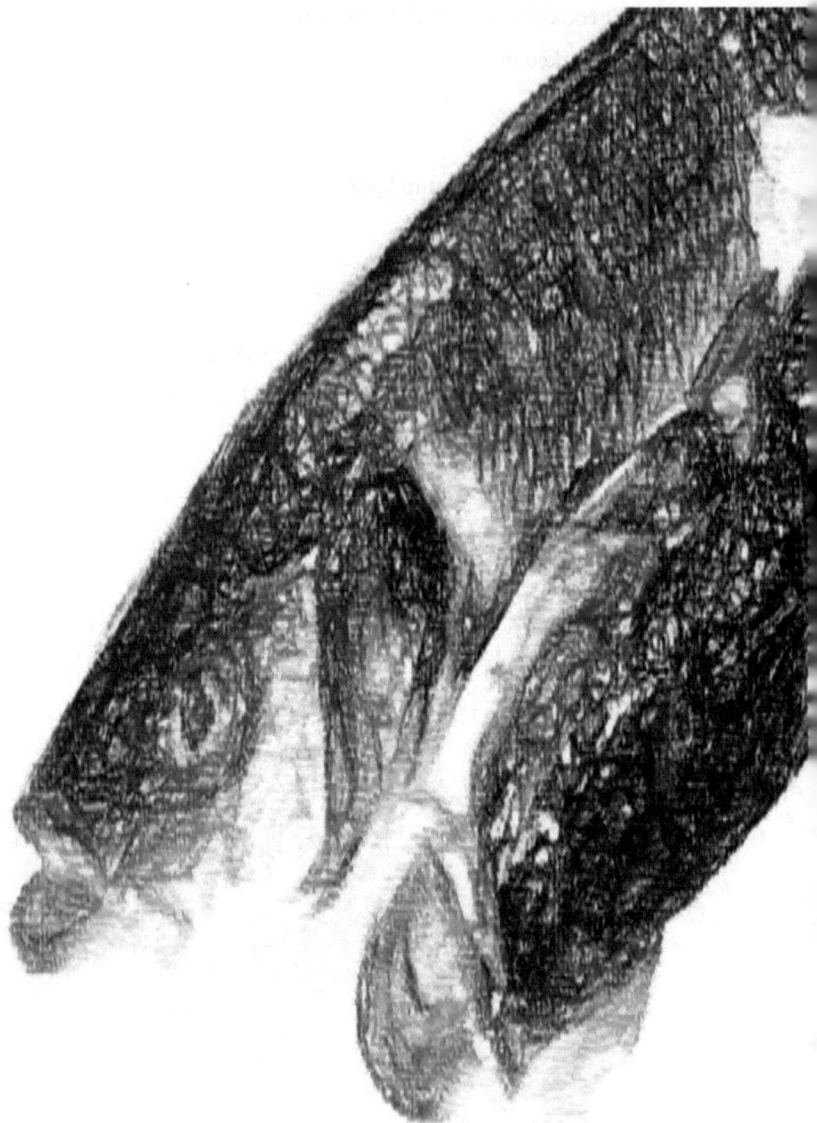

- 51 -

worms

parasites wriggling in the fish flesh
in the belly of the men too
making an intolerable existence even worse
sea maggots
burrowing when exposed to the light
feeding
sucking
popping full of blood when dug out
twisted n corkscrewed
some things he wished he could unsee
felt them crawling even when they were gone
men scratching themselves with nails and knives
making some mess
like he was warned
he knew if he started scratching
no matter how itchy it got
that would be the end.

- 52 -

lack of silage

another forgettable morning
one old fella was whistling a familiar tune
had heard it down the mines countless times before
it flowed out of him as if he was a wee robin
Jack felt the rise of an urge to join in
feeling a shell of happiness breaking out from the depths
but no tune would flow out his flaked gub
half a huff of dejected air was all
and he settled back to the misery of the fish
toenails crushing against those small boots
fingers pulsating
eyes stinging with salt
the emptiness in his belly
expanding with each passing minute
few things affect a man more than hunger
cant think straight
irritable beyond sense
cant focus or concentrate
or even carry a thought for more than a few seconds
add thirst into the mix

broken sleep

never ending cold winds

rain

sleet

back breaking work

with pieces of the men being shed every day

and youve got a rancid soup on a ship

all stirred by the gaffers hatred

overflowing into the sea

turning it to vinegar.

- 53 -

far far away

fog so thick you couldnt see your hand in front of you
hardly a pinprick of light
then sheets of rain would come down
and disappear as if by a switch
the days followed this pattern for eight long mornings
floating on seas of hot tar
ice licking lips n armpits
the fish filled the deck
and met their fate over n over again
conversations faded to black
not as much as a hiss of breath anymore
he tuned out under the blanket of water
and always thought of home
a land long lost to only memory.

- 54 -

night divine

Christmas day
he would get a good wash n put on his best clothes
had a roaring coal fire on in the living room
and played with his boy
carved him soldiers every year
and they would add the new additions to their platoon
then set the table
big families all around but theirs was tiny in comparison
just the three of them and her maw
but he preferred it that way
turnip soup to start
mince n tatties
then apple pie n thick custard
oh ya dancer
he would be full for weeks after
they would all sit on the couch
and he would read to the boy on his knee
sip some brandy
and listen to music on the wireless
could taste the happiness of the day
long into the cold of January.

- 55 -

open

regret always settled on your chest at night
nights when you couldnt sleep
chalky memories crumbling inside your skull
and the rubble gathered in your throat
pieces fell
grabbing and consuming fibres
until you were a dead weight with wet eyes
body stuck in the present
mind trapped in the past
no way of scalping the skin off either
just a long exhausting wait for morning
sleep only nightmares
he took out his gutting knife
and without thinking
carved her name into the wood
he lay back and stared at the darkness above
knife resting by his throat.

- 56 -

memories of violence

an earless man
one of the fellas that worked on the nets
was muttering to himself
and descended into a fit of shouting
the gaffers men told him to shut it
but he kept on going n going
getting louder
he was shaking n spitting out bubbles of foam
they were all going to hell
and he didnt want to die
wanted off the ship
wanted his maw
tears streaming
he was holding onto legs n pleading
choking
face turning red
eyes bulging
no words were calming him down
needed to go home

just needed to go home
he kept on screaming and screaming
the gaffer appeared with a handkerchief under his chin
he spoke with folded arms n sunken eyebrows
but nothing but the mans screams could be heard
the gaffer signalled for everyone to relax
and disappeared with a smile
the seal club returned
bleeding in the rain
it took several blows to return the silence
the earless creature lay wriggling on the deck
before being helped to the bunks
Jack never saw him again.

– 57 –

cold soup

the stove wasnt working
it was that or the crooked nosed bastard cook
couldnt be arsed to turn it on again
soup as if it was scooped straight out of the sea for dinner
second time that week
ice tatties
carrots you had to suck cos you couldnt bite through them
men ate with their hands
and wiped dripping fingers on their hair n beards
not many things worse for morale than waiting all day for a warm
meal
and getting one colder than the gaffers heart
that piece of shite had roasting hot stew
and a warm buttered roll though
washed himself with a basin of blood warm water too
and his pinked skin made sure the men knew how hot it was
as they all fell apart
he was still piling on the weight
coming out his office sweating as their skins iced over
he wasnt eating cold soup
that was for certain.

– 58 –

breathing

when he was just born
Jack used to check that wee Jackie was breathing
several times a night
such a fragile thing
a tiny wee beastie of a boy
if he couldnt see his chest moving
he would put Erins glasses by his nose
and look for condensation
their whole world
petrified that something bad would happen to him
had this lingering feeling
that he was in trouble long before he was
didnt know where it came from
beyond words when he left them
far far beyond.

- 59 -

celebration

old swollen hands sat on his bunk after dinner with a smile
and produced half a bottle of whisky
his nose metallic in the pale lamp light

shhh

found it in the kitchen n snuck it out
no one paying attention to an old yin
asked Jack if he fancied a wee celebratory drink
cos it was his sixtieth birthday
he poured out a handful of porridge oats on the sheet
and they chewed n drank
toasted n toasted
blethering in whispers
words of home came out the old mans mouth
and drifted in the cold
before falling like a feather into the puddles at their feet
Jack felt he could pick them up
shake them

and read them back
taste the bitterness of his own regrets
old swollen hands was a crofter from the Highlands
the last of his five brothers alive
wife dead from consumption the winter before last
daughter moved to Edinburgh to work in the grain mill
signed up for the Arctic to pay for her wedding
he had worn photos of them in his pocket
eased them out n placed into a trembling hand
like they were the most expensive diamonds in all the world
milkblue veins pulsating in wrists
Jack smiled with twisted insides
what he would have given for a photo of Erin n wee Jackie
in that moment
everything.

- 60 -

abandoned

Jack traced the carving of her name with brittle fingers

left alone

with that empty room

bedsheets still not washed since the last time hed slept there

every morning before breakfast

she sat on their boys empty bed

he didnt dare join her

even when she asked

just sat in the living room smoking

and stared out the window

she was alone now in that empty house

son gone

husband too

broke his heart all over again thinking about her back there

the thought boiled vinegar and blistering on his tongue

unable to be spat or swallowed

pressed his eyes until yellow rings circled the dark.

- 61 -

lost

he woke up hungover n cotton mouthed
old swollen hands was frantic
looking under bunks n bothering anyone that got near him
jawseams grouted with black spittle

Ive lost them
have you seen them
my photos
have you seen them
somebody has taken my photos of Grace n Mary
somebody must have taken them
I always have them in my pillowcase
always
but theyre no there
and Ive searched everywhere
they were right here when I went to sleep
right here
mind I showed you them
mind

have you seen them
Jack helped him look
but found nothing but dust n mould
old swollen hands lunged into the next room
burst into another
face getting redder n wetter by the second
asking men to empty their pockets
the whistle was drowning out his voice
grabbed men by the collar
pleaded and pleaded all day on the cans to anyone who would listen
at dinner he was silent
eyes dripping
wept himself to sleep.

- 62 -

working underground

never had to consider the weather
that was the main thing
didnt matter what was going on up there
it was always the same day down there
heavy rain brought with it muddy boots n conveyor belts
but that didnt change much at all
descending out of the suns light
and coming back when it was dark every season bar summer
felt strange seeing that almighty ball on days of rest
he would sit in the garden with a book n let it warm his face
the sound of birds that werent caged canaries
the wind swaying tall green trees n grass that needed cut
she would sit by him
stomach growing
telling how she now knew the name if it was a boy
he smiled
held her hand
in a matter of days their first child would be born.

nothing

as they ate their supper
the gaffer was red nosed n swinging a whisky bottle
he stood on a table n spat on the roof
a string of flaking warts showed from under his collarbone

know nothing
most of youse green boys know nothing
mammys blue eyed boys eh
nothing I tell youse
nothing of hardship
nothing of Fritz
moaning about sore hands n cold feet
a bunch of Jessies is what youse are
weaker than old women
try picking limbs out the battlefield
try running into a hail of bullets on the orders of a lunatic
and have your wee brothers head blown off
and being showered in their blood
try that for size eh

he smashed the bottle n laughed with wet red eyes
last chance
show me tomorrow that youse are real men
show me
youse are well looked after on here
very fucking well
Ive seen to it myself that youse are
afraid of a wee bit hard work and a nippy wind
a disgrace
thats what youse are
a fucking disgrace
show me youse are real men tomorrow
I will not have cowards on my ship
that I fucking promise youse
cowards can jump off the sides
and swim to their icy grave.

– 64 –

a spray of flies

air black
thick with coal dust
the heat
the noise
machines roaring like dragons
but it was peaceful at the surface
ears ringing until silence took over once again
shielded his eyes from a white sun
a teuchter fella had appeared at the entrance of the pit
had on the finest dark blue suit he had ever laid eyes on
a thick smile n black glasses over eyes like cigarette ash
hands full of crisp pamphlets
was only going to certain places in Scotland
strong men were needed for the chance of a lifetime
and he had heard great things about their wee village
a fierce reputation of being hard workers
the hardest in all of Scotland he said
the promise was five times the wages of their pit work
guaranteed hours and an iron clad pension

a fat bonus each time their contract was fulfilled
hours were not as long either
no unpaid work getting to the coal face
as much good whisky as they could drink on board
as much good food as they could eat
real fine scran made by a proper cook
want for nothing
and back before they knew it
not want to leave

he wrapped his finger flapping from a rusty can cut
and got back to scooping out bones from flesh
eejits the lot of them
most of the men were grey
more life left in what was being thrown back to the sea
a fair few were still sooking fish skin n eyes
for some well needed calories
he avoided it as it only added to his thirst
by the time the bucket of drinking rainwater reached his lips
after passing through fifty before it
it was as salty as the sea
rain days were seen as a bonus in that sense
with water running from his hair
the balance of being soaked made both horrific options.

- 65 -

waiting on dinner

one of the last to eat
the cabin smelt of raw cow shite
soup was lukewarm n vinegary again
but finished every last drop
pieces of rotten apples shovelled over to the table
he bit into the soft brown flesh
and it clung to his teeth
core and all
the men ate them like starved animals
stinking out his kitchen the cook said
all had to go
he poured a bucketful on the floor
and it was gone in mere seconds
Jack went back to his bunk with two wet apples
and a blue skinned orange
and guarded them like a dragon on gold.

- 66 -

snow

littered the sky
and mixed with the beams of moonlight
arms like melted branches
hands like January flower heads
they were dead eyed snowmen sifting through scales n bones
the red headed brothers drooped
canning at the speed of a slow motion picture
the gaffers main men burst into life
and kicked n lashed n kicked n lashed
no one was to give up because of a few drops of snow
no one
nearly done for the day
nearly fucking done so just keep going
keep fucking going
blood ran through shouts n screams n inked the snow
Jack caught a stray blow aimed for another
licked the space were a solid tooth once lived
the taste of liquid iron
the commotion ended and all fell to a whisper

the last net raised and opened

instead of relieving themselves overboard

the older men all agreed to piss themselves

kept them warm

the fish smell masked it from their soiled clothing

but they were nearly done

and not just with that days shift

heading back to Scotland in mere days was what spilled out

over the worst of it

blethering at supper confirmed they were finally on their way home

men talked about what they were doing as soon as they got their wages

what they would eat

drink

buy for their wives n weans

have roasting hot baths n wash the salt n stench away

all of them certain of one thing

they were never getting on a ship again

Jack was trying not to think that far ahead

but his thoughts sprinted home

to her.

human heat

plenty of beds
but men were sleeping in the same bunk for warmth
the smell from his own skin made him heave
never mind anyone elses
grease n soft splinters in fingernails
eyes peeled for an extra blanket instead
old swollen hands still whispering to the night
about his missing photos
emptiness was growing like a cancer
consuming
he was sinking
and had little grip to pull himself back out
but they were heading home
finally heading home
he had just about enough left to make it.

- 68 -

a meeting

canning was slammed to a halt not long after breakfast
and the engine was cut
they were all ushered to sit by a tangle of nets
a blur of withered morning sunshine beating on faces
the gaffer smashed a bottle off the side to get their attention
productivity was too low after a promising start
far too low
this meant pay had to be suspended until this was rectified
if he wasnt getting paid
how could he pay them
how
however he believed in them
every last one of them
and that they would be able to turn things around
the weather was turning n getting darker earlier
but instead of turning back
they were heading for deeper waters
this was the only option to ensure they would all get paid
and paid well

they had to go where the fish were
and no one knew fish like he did
anyone who disagreed could swim home at any time
Jack swallowed
saw his reflection in a salty puddle by his feet
a black eye that glistened like freshly cut coal
glass shards shook inside his belly as he stood
trembling back to his position on the line.

- 69 -

the wretched

as morning broke
the moustached fella with the salt tang didnt move
hed been up all night wailing with cramps
scratching his skin raw
shitting pints of blood
that dripped down the wooden boards of his top bunk
the stench was unbearable
like curdled yoghurt hatched from rotten eggs
around his face resembled that of the skin on boiled milk
an old yin tried explaining to the gaffers men
that he was too sick n needed to rest
leave him be was best
give him a wee sleep
and he would maybe make the afternoon

up
come on
up
weve no room for shirkers on this ship

you know the rules
get up
if one of youse gets to lie in
youse will all want a lie in
and it would create havoc
come on you
get up
youll be fine once you start working
we all feel the same
youll get a good sleep tonight
up you get
get up
GET UP NOW
NOW
I SAID NOW

hired to squeeze out every last drop of labour
they didnt listen
when he couldnt stand after being pulled from his bed
they rained belts n boots into him until they exhausted themselves
Jack was held back by the red headed brothers
would be next if he did anything
the moustached fella was already dead.

- 70 -

carrots

the cook had grown silent during supper
his wobbly arms twitched behind his back
thin hairs trapped in grease struggling to poke out his neck
his usual back n forth with men asking for more food
was only one way
his usual tired repertoire of

there are rations on here
and as much as I want to give youse more I cant
I cant
I just cant
complain to the gaffer not me
this food has to last

was replaced by guttural grunts
Jack took his wee serving of porridge n bread
and kept his mouth shut
a netter behind him tried to sneak his hand over
to steal an extra piece of buttered bread

and the cook pounced into life
grabbed him by the elbow
and slammed a meat cleaver across his fingers
four of them fell to the floor like chopped carrots

thats my final warning
how many times have youse been telt
eh
how many times
Ive had enough of you stinking bastards
enough
I am a professional
Ive worked on many a ship
I deserve respect
the screaming netter n the fingers were scooped up
and ushered out
black blood puddled around the chair legs
the gaffer sauntered in and burst out laughing.

- 71 -

fury

rage with no direction but to himself
it swelled in all the men
pulsating blue under their skin
the gaffer was without doubt a sadistic bastard
nothing on that ship was clearer
and he was only getting worse
knowing they were powerless to do anything
and if they did
they would have done all that work for nothing
all those days n nights folding their bodies to muck
more n more nights Jack would go to bed seething
trembling with anger
and nowhere for it to go
but to burst into his own watery nightmares.

- 72 -

alive with noise

didnt know what day it was
or month
all he knew it was another dark night on a ship to hell
heading deeper n deeper into unclaimed darkness
never realised how comfy his bed was at home
until he continuously slept on one harder than concrete
metal bricks
blankets all wires
no different to sleeping on a dirt road in winter
he brushed hair out from his face
and twisted
lay on his back
milky green light growing against the windowpanes
needed to sleep to soothe the poison out of his lungs
pleaded for it
but again
sleep wasnt for coming
men talking n shouting
some laughing like gibbering wrecks

Stoneyetts had nothing on that ship

nothing

his throat tickled n needed water

tried swallowing but his mouth was dried out

rolled over on his side n placed his head on the wall

pain rippled

the laughter and coarse voices enclosed around his ears

kept swallowing

trying to wet his throat

sleep

the voices

his throat

pain spiralling to every inch that touched the bed

and nothing could be done

nothing

but to endure.

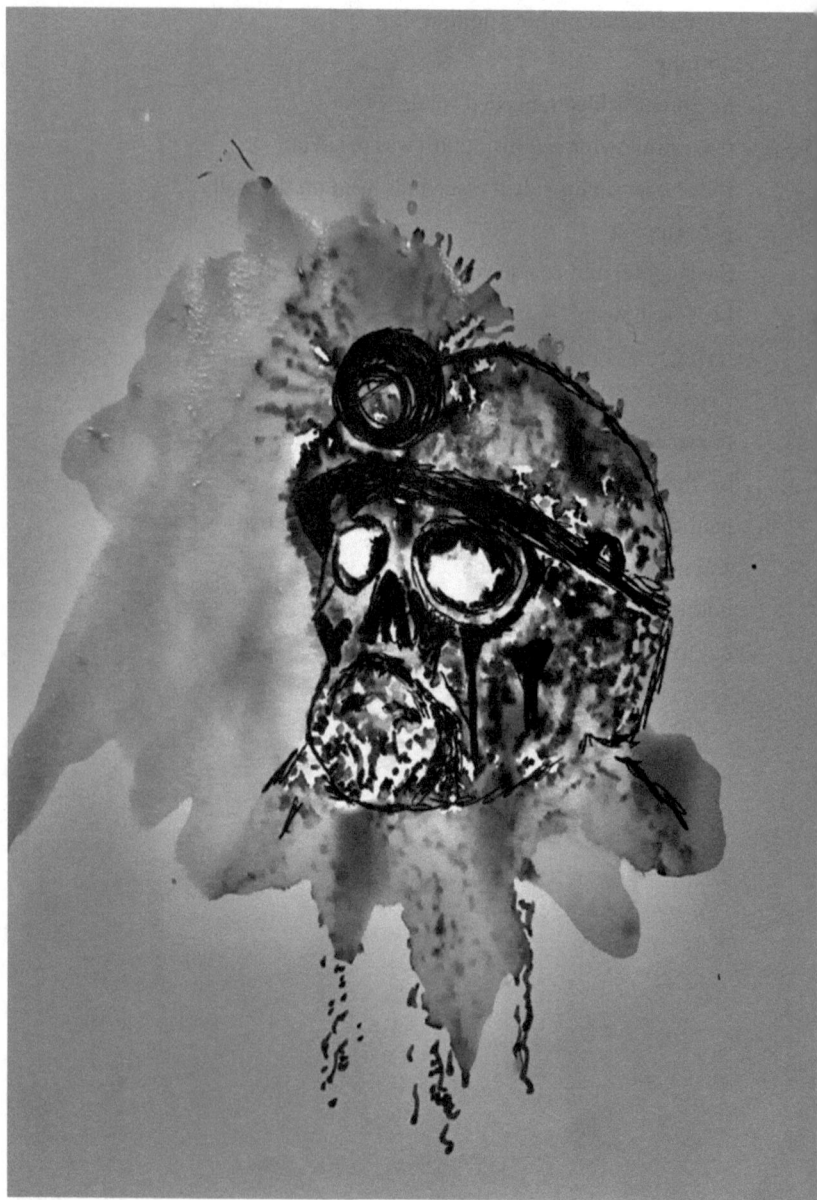

callous landlords

sixteen years n seven days old
after five long ones down the pit
Jack knew every noise had a purpose
and nothing could be ignored as disaster was never far away
the old yins told him they could hear it
and he had to hear it too
that was a must
or he would be dead at the first sign of danger
the day shift was almost over
the meagre beams of Davy lamps
ready to be passed on to the next fella
a rumble like thunder was enough to pause all men
poked their heads out
the second noise had them dropping tools
and bursting a lung to get out
a shower of dust turned to a roar
and roofs collapsed all around
he sprinted with the rest of the leading pack
bodies pushing against bodies

panic trembling in faces n limbs
the dust created a fog so thick it ate all
suffocating
hands searching with crawling eyes for the light
scrambling through the tunnels as they collapsed
and collapsed
voices of trapped men screaming for help behind him
screaming
screaming
never looked back
couldnt
just kept running n crawling n tearing through the dark
limbs at breaking point
beams n girders snapping like twigs
kept on running n running
mouth eyes n nose full of dirt n dust
soot drooling from faces
running
pulling himself through the smaller holes
with cracked and bleeding fingernails
men hanging out the cage as it dragged them up
he collapsed in the early winter sunshine
sweat n tears nipping eyes n cuts
gasping

gasping for breath
sirens wailed for help
weeping in the dying sun

a new tunnel was already being dug at dawn
and the water at the bottom of the shaft pumped out
men braver than him sent back down the next morning
to retrieve the bodies
pink froth bubbled out from holes in their ribcages
blackened skin n torn limbs resting on stretchers
back to work was the order once the machines had gone
and the departed had been carted out
the owners couldnt cease production after every accident
could they
Scotland relied on them for heat
for warmth
an essential service
and that was what had to be honoured
that was what those brave men would have wanted
the lifeless were carried off into the weeds
new faces already hired and in place of the dead
any of the survivors wanting to quit more than welcome to.

- 74 -

lies of the ship

he sat on the edge of his bed
and wrapped a bandage around new cuts in his palm
empty bunks
still stained with sweat from their former occupants
far from the early days when men were doubling up
and blankets were scarce
thick lines of water ran down the walls
drips pooled into puddles of grease
the rot was swelling
eating the air
his cabin stank of the vinegar mopped on the floor
but the blood stains n vomit were still caked into the fibres
he turned n faced the ceiling
things were starting to make sense
the gaffer never intended to pay them all did he
maybe not any of them
it twigged when he realised every one of them was on their first run
every last one
no returners

a brand new crew

bastards

worthless contracts that rotted muscle

bent bones

work them until their bodies gave out

and use the excuse they have broken contracts

less men to pay

more profits to be had

there wasnt a shortage of desperate men in Scotland

ready to be exploited

and they fucking knew it.

– 75 –

all for nothing

everything was gritting
scraping under the skin
wet mouths breathed near ears
men snoring from all angles was too much to bear
wrapped in a sea of mud
footsteps on the soiled boards
the snapping of knuckles
and stale breath blowing into hands
pains he never thought existed birthed into life on that ship
toenails peeling off inside boots
cartilage cracking and crumbling
skin on fire without a slither of heat
if he had any energy
he would explode with pain that was foaming outwards
instead
he poured out of the bunk
and into the white cold for another shift
kept in mind it was all for nothing if he didnt
all for nothing

forced that to the forefront of his thoughts

he was getting paid

had to be

no chance he was going back with nothing

was taking back every shilling to Erin

no chance of that not happening

no chance

was still the dead of night when they had to get up

and out into the raw elements

the promised sun not yet ready to appear for a long while

and that yellow beam faded to a few grey hours at best.

- 76 -

rewards

night sandpapered the remains of the day away
and left the sky blood red
lamps glowed n hearts sank
much harder working in shadows
and the temperature dropped to unthinkable levels
how there was still a decent crew left
was a testament to how determined they all were
a wild determination flowing through them
that they would not go home with nothing
the gaffer appeared holding a cup of boiling hot tea

right listen up men
this is important
youse need to make up for the dead n the invalids
if we get behind the canning
too much fish will go to waste
and that means less money for all of us
Im more than happy to give youse time off
if youse work for it

more than happy
give youse a good days rest
and time to let off some steam
I ken youse are needing it
Im not blind
but give me three strong days
full days
thats all Im asking for
work the worth of two men
and I will pay you two mens wages

Jack didnt bother to even raise his head
to the latest motivational speech
felt melted n refroze to the deck
waiting for the night lamps to heat
turn him into water
and pour back down the stairs
to the weeping n gnashing of teeth.

- 77 -

the haar

another morning opened its eyes on the scalloped seas
sea mist was devouring the ship once more
the haar he heard it being called by an east coast accent
couldnt see the man in front of him
could hardly see his own hands
cocooned n waiting for time to be called
surely he couldnt expect them to work blind
the gaffer was waving his arms
screaming n screaming at it to fuck off
and that they were haemorrhaging money again
as if mist was something he could talk to
reason with
exactly how the men felt about him
he was the haar
and nothing n nobody could reason with him
not even as they worked blind on the edge of the world
and he knew men were freezing
falling over the side
getting sick

dying
thought about taking his knife
and ramming it into the back of his neck
wouldnt see it coming
and was what he deserved
probably not the only one with that idea.

- 78 -

cards

the brief glow of the sun had long faded n set once more

night lamps swaying with a fresh wind

dinner had been getting later n later each night

the mist had just about lifted

time still hadnt been called

even though it was promised to be early for their previous hard work

the weather was threatening to turn again

another card game in the gaffers office

as the men worked their fingers red

cigar smoke belched from under the wet window

laughter

as much as they all hated that fat wee bastard

none hoped he would lose this time

didnt want to feel the wrath

his chamber pot launched at them was the nicest it would be

each shout n jeer n oily handprint on the window folded stomachs

the door burst open n breaths were held

he came out with a smile stretched over his face

and spat into the dark water

inspected a can

and whispered to a cabin boy

Jack swallowed

pockets of relief fizzled

and the regular dull ache took control once more

nose was blocked n air hard to reach

but could still smell the cold guts of the poor fish

like the coal dust

it would never leave him

he expected the gaffer to finally call time

but he didnt

just glanced at his pocket watch

and headed back inside

was long past midnight before that whistle sounded.

eleven

wandered through the glen

warped purple n blue plants wrapped around tall tree stumps

legs sinking into wet mud

his mother walking on

as his feet were grabbed by unseen hands

and pulled under

sank to his knees

called out for help

but no words formed

she kept walking

not looking back

he kept sinking

past his waist

chest

neck

chin

nose

eyes

awoke in darkness
was like trying to see through a soaked blanket
the morning whistle still to sound
rubbed his face n held knees to his chest
was never allowed to visit her
that kind of hospital wasnt a place for weans
she would be back when she was all better
granny would take care of youse
no need to worry
but granny only took care of the girls
her wrinkled smile
always looked as if it was held in place by needles
he was a godless wee devil
who drove her daughter to madness
only hate radiated from her eyes
her broken heart
drifted apart from his sisters who sided with their granny
a man at eleven
groomed for the underworld
black gold awaiting.

- 80 -

fragments

weeks upon weeks upon weeks passed
an onslaught of near identical days
boiling on the edge of the horizon
solid floats of ice tapping the sides of the ship
and icicles dripping from their own bones too
under urine soaked fur
the men hauling in the nets were brittle
and less than half of what they were in Aberdeen
dipping the last of the bread into curdled soup
with vacant looks frozen on their faces
sour bones
stench of dried sweat n stale breath
shirt collars stained raw with old blood
Jack sipped his share of lime cordial n shivered

there were worse ships to work on an old timer whispered
as if reading his thoughts

hairless
skin like leather

blisters bubbling on the edges of his lips

at least this one wasnt being shot at he said

or bombed

they generally got fed on here

enough

no

but it was better than nothing

better than a lot of circumstances

and they were allowed some kip to recharge

seen worse

felt worse

and if they did die

die out on a boat drifting over an ocean full of ice n silence

what a beautiful place to go.

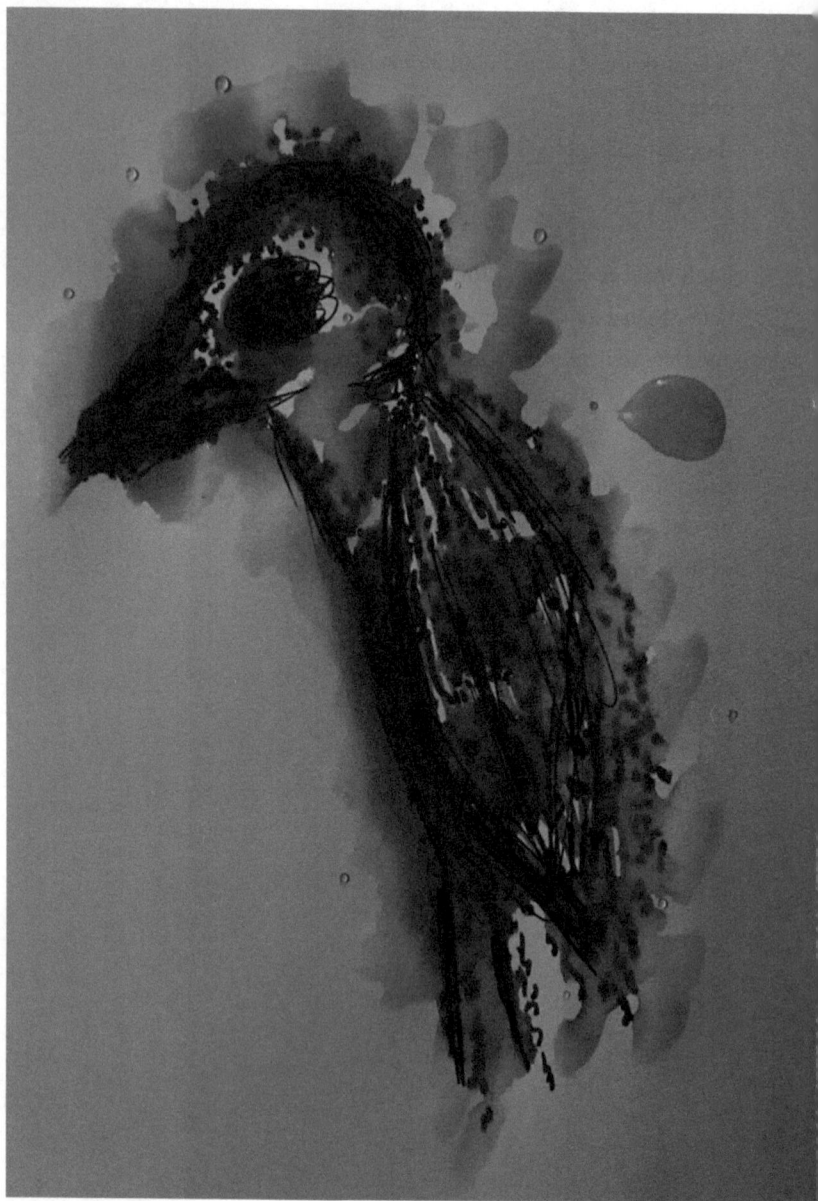

- 81 -

broken

heard a faint chirping for a few nights
thought it was from the engine
poked his head under the bunk out of curiosity
and saw a wee seabird cowering in a corner
he managed to coax it out
and lifted it onto his bed
its wings were mangled n it had a starved look
didnt know what to do
held it in his hands to warm it
and fed it some crumbs from his beard
that lingered from his buttered bread dinner
it let out a few chirps n nestled into his neck
exhaustion swallowed them both
by morning the bird was a frozen lump by his cheek.

- 82 -

fading

the dregs of sunlight warmed his face
the men grew mute and worked in silence
not even the odd whistle came out
every man that surrounded him had a wet cough
dripping nose
never felt like any of them got to dry out from the rain
wet clothes
damp spreading in their lungs
rot settled in their skin
pale light smouldered over the black sizzle of waves
bitterness welled
choking thoughts
a snake of anxiety crawled
pushing into his chest n coiled around his heart
had to survive this
had to survive
and get back on land
get home
the thought of never seeing her again
was punishment enough

not being able to say sorry for leaving

abandoning her

was a rancid ulcer in itself

never mind the punishing work n weather

he spat

nothing but a bubble of foam came out

and stayed on his bottom lip

gritted teeth

he was making it back

not dying on a ship

that made money selling fucking cheap canned fish.

– 83 –

another gone

drift nets all but empty
fear seeping out of the ships skin
the thin veil between life n death
falling into a silky puddle on the floor
the gaffer lashing all in his path
time was called as the fat fucker planned a new route
they went down to warm by the engine
no sign of the cabin boys for four days
both were well fed n bunked with the gaffers men
faces full but empty
late morning the boy with soapy eyes appeared with a brush
questions about where his wee pal was shot down n drowned
the wean didnt open his gub
but his whimpering told the tale as good as words
at supper a prayer was held
the missing boy had slipped overboard
drunk
broke into the gaffers whisky cabinet n filled his belly
a thief and worst still a heathen
they had to pray for his soul
Jack sneered.

beneath the wonder

nothing untouched by the winds sharp hands
waiting on time being called
counting the seconds with his jaw
but the work kept piling
and piling
and piling
a luminous green mist floated in the sky
then was swallowed by thin clouds
and all was grey above once more
men rambled about what they had seen
ghosts of the dead lost at sea
poison
sea gas
they all had an explanation
Jack was more concerned with the dark blood in his shite
and hoping he wouldnt be the next to collapse
black clouds of flies danced above their food
scabs like knitted flowers covering exposed n unexposed skin
were they already dead and in hell

was that light giving them the go ahead to sail to Hades
the fuck he knew anymore
time
where they were
had been
were going
had lost all meaning
purple eyed men
gutting fish on black water
that was it.

- 85 -

my son

a dream of his handsome wee face soured
flesh came apart from the bone
and he screamed
screamed
screamed

predawn
cold sweat ran from his neck
none of the men awake
Jack sat on the edge of the bunk with his head in his hands
the worst thing was thinking about his wee body in that grave
surrounded by darkness
alone
decaying
his wee face no longer what it was
skin turning colder n colder
grey

my son
my sweet boy

come back to us
let me feel the warmth
just once more
thats all I need
never stop waiting for that day.

- 86 -

dignity lost

a smaller haul from the nets didnt ease the workload
with worker numbers almost half what they left with
there wasnt much time to spare
hands got so cold he felt they would shatter
tried everything
gloves were allowed but only rubber ones
any other kind got soaked
and in the way of the canning
never got a pair and neither did the others
only seen the gaffers cronies with them on
tried sitting on his palms between catches
tucking fingers under armpits
rubbing them together
making fists
wrapping them in torn bedsheets
sucking them
but his gub was no coal fire
and that did fuck all
except make him gag from the taste of fish guts n wet salt

felt like he was on fire a layer beneath the skin it was so cold
last resort
held them out by the side n pissed for some heat
but the stream came out as warm as an outdoor tap
freezing inside n out
wiped dripping palms on his trousers
and felt the glare of witnesses
reduced to a disgrace of a human.

- 87 -

enough

whispers of a mutiny spread in dark bunks that night

and breached the waters

the men finally had enough

and something had to be done before they all died

there was no other option

no amount of money was worth another days work

a lisped voice rose

the gaffer could be willing to negotiate the working terms

and maybe the eating situation too

if we showed him we were serious I bet he would

hes not a man that can be negotiated with another said

could ask him

you go ask him then

I will

go on then

I will

what are you waiting for

Im going

fucking go then you weedy prick
and quit kidding yourself on
the lisped voice left
in less than ten minutes he was back
eye socket swollen
mouth dripping with blood
the mutiny was happening the next morning
and all had to prepare.

- **88** -

brewing

wind was singing in the cracks

nothing but that song stirred as morning turned to dust

the men who said they would lead the mutiny

all waited on each other to start it

and none did

waited

and waited

waited till the stars came out

then the idea turned to ash

needed to be better organised

after supper whispers spread once more

a tall fella had nominated himself as the first domino

he would make a stance and the rest were to follow

worked at the nets

was going to call the gaffer over

toss him into the sea

and the rest of them had to rush his men

soon two three four men had specific jobs to do

hushed voices extinguished for the night

and all sleep was silent.

- 89 -

bath

returning from the pit in the winter months
arms n shoulders ached
fire on in the living room
a steaming basin of water and a sponge beside it
waiting
dinner bubbling on the stove
haggis neeps n tatties fogging the kitchen window
she would smile
wrap her arms around him
they would sit by the fire n she would wash his back
the warmth running
soothing
taking away all the hours under the ground
and back to the mortal realm.

- 90 -

a grass

black morning shadows

he poured out of bed with a thumping heart

and scaled the steps

all eyes were darting

the tall man was nowhere to be seen by the nets

the gaffer greeted them with a smile on his face

the amount of times he had goosegogs thinking they could overthrow him was laughable

he skipped about like a wee lassie playing hopscotch

broke a sweepers arm

and the snap echoed off the wet wooden floor

pain hissed out his mouth

they would all be snapped

if they didnt get back to fucking work

dinner was a half portion for the next week

if he even heard the smallest whisper about a mutiny again

it would be even less going forward

hollow men with hollow bones

a grass was amongst them

eyes burned into eyes.

- 91 -

nightfall

evening wind on damp faces
the gaffer swung out of his office chewing on a pork chop
his warm mouth wet with venom
smashed an empty whisky bottle against the anchor
and laughed as the glass sprayed the nearest men

the deepest circle of hell is reserved for mutineers
are you not God fearing men
huh
does Gods wrath hold no fear for youse

Jack swallowed as the gaffer pranced around the deck
with his mining boots on
eager for one of them to show any sign of discontent
the gaffer unbuckled his trousers

you look cold boy
I should heat you up before you freeze eh
took a piss over the back and neck of the dark eyed man

he hung his head n didnt move
a thick yellow stench filling their nostrils

that will heat you up good and proper
good
this is good
I see weve all had a good think today n reached a consensus
good choice
a godly choice you could say eh
right
enough childish games
lets get back to work
we are all here to make money
I shouldnt need to be out here telling you this
should I
your faces are putting me off my tea
another wee hour or so
and I will think about calling time.

- 92 -

solidarity

not enough porridge for dinner
he got a half scraping from a burnt pot and told to fuck off
gulped it down before someone grabbed it
news that the kitchen was closed filtered back to the empty mouths
and violence washed over the room
he hid under a table as the cook was leathered
and heading for death
until the gaffers men poured in to sand the fire
brown n grey fish guts in warm water was soon provided
if they didnt know that starving men can turn beyond wild
they did now
anger at the front of all thoughts
on tongues
in throats
Jack crawled out n went back to his bunk
icicles running with orange rust in the lamplight by his bed
no one speaking
solidarity long since wavered.

- 93 -

dark sorrow

griefs insatiable hunger
tried everything to blank out the pain after their boy got sick
pneumonia
couldnt save him
floated into the pit the next morning
hardly able to draw breath
the drink made things worse
noticed more
only saw stale pints and overflowing ashtrays
in what used to be a place of comfort
the filth inside n out
took all the novels that were dumped in the social club home
and tried to escape
Hemingway n Scott did nothing but paint bleak reminders of war
of all his fathers letters from the trenches
of his maws screaming and subsequent trip to Stoneyetts
the mental asylum that she never reappeared from
the world was a rancid soup
curdling
the only good thing left he ignored
she looked too much like him
couldnt bear much more than a glance.

– 94 –

limbs

a scream echoed along the corridor
stopped the men mid bite at dinner
one of the gaffers men burst in
sweat dripping from his forehead
Jack was grabbed at random
and told to report to the gaffers office
another picked out n told the same thing
he stuffed the mouldy bread into his mouth
and chewed on the walk over
knew he wouldnt be able to eat after
heard what happens from the last men that were volunteered
the gaffer greeted them with gritted teeth n spat
a thin fella with frog eyes was squirming on the floor
trousers rolled up to the knee
his feet were dark green n peeling slices of grey sponge

right
take an arm each n hold him down
if he moves I will end up cutting one of youse

so make sure he doesnt
got it

can I get just a sip
please I need a sip
just a wee sip
even just to wet my mouth
I just need a fucking sip
just a fu

youll get fuck all whisky boy
youll bleed out if you do
its for your own good
now stop fucking moving
and shut your geggy

frog eyes bit down on a belt
Jack knelt n took hold of his left arm
the gaffer slid out a saw
and positioned it halfway down the shin bone
frog eyes screams mixed with the tearing of wet flesh
and dry bone
told youse to look after your feet the day we boarded
didnt I
this spreads fast
only way to save him
only way
Ill hang these up as a reminder to youse all

looked like he took pleasure in the scene
smile widening as the saw went deeper
black bubbles of blood running
the saw spraying the walls with every stroke
a lamb like bleat was the last sound his mouth made
frog eyes passed out as the gaffer snipped the hanging flesh
tossed the foot into a bucket n started on the other
Jack felt sweat running down his back
eyes watered
the room spun

the next morning frog eyes was gone

didnt make it one of the gaffers men said
didnt make it.

- 95 -

smouldering

days
weeks
and still nothing of the mutiny
but steam rose in the dead of night
hot chains of breath
he kept out of the new plans
as the whispers spread n caught fire
out of fear
hated himself even more for that
sickness in his throat
felt brittle
eggshell skin
a fever was eating him from the inside
and there was no way to stop it
just wanted to get back home to her
back to where he belonged.

- 96 -

rain turned to sleet

crisp noses ran
men took turns to sneak into the engine room for a heat
steam puffed from clothes n clumps of hair
the boards creaked
and the deck filled until they were squatting in icy puddles
he got a rare break from canning
and was handed a wire brush
swept as much water as his frozen arms would allow
but it didnt make much difference
as the waves n sky refilled more than went over
the gaffer only called time on the shift when his product
was in extreme danger of being washed overboard
packed it away n waited for supper
they all owed him overtime
that was all he talked about
overtime
overtime
pathetic runts
weak

not a decent man between them
Jack went to his bunk
dinner would be an hour was the word
and if anyone complained it would be cancelled
he stripped out his wet clothes
and hung them by the lantern
curled up under the blanket
closed his eyes for a short nap
when he opened them
it was long into morning
was even too late for breakfast.

space

the shift started in the pitch black
but there was a delay with the first catch
Jack waited
savouring every rested second
long blinks
thought he would feel hungrier than he did
he stood and stared at the stars
stared until his eyes watered n burned
salt and ash running from his nose
chattering teeth
and the belching engine below the only sounds

if we ever leave this world
and get to whatever exists out there
it will be a tragic day
not one of celebration
as we will just ruin whatever we find
mine it dry
build belching factories for the weak to waste away in

and gut their oceans

paying for it all with the blood of the lowly workers

as always

the only winners in any of it

the rich and the greedy

no one else

and that wont change on another planet.

another accident

before the dark sank
and the black winds descended
a netter with a hooked nose screamed
as his arm was caught in a launch
ripped right out from the pit
sprayed like it was champagne at a horse racing victory
the men had to hold him down n tried to stem the wound
but there was fuck all that could be done
he was white eyed in no time
old swollen hands said he wouldve no doubt died of shock
and had a heart attack
the gaffer gave them five minutes to clean the deck
so the fish wouldnt be contaminated
the remainder of the body was fed to the sea
not as much as a kind word to send him off.

- 99 -

branding

the gaffer burst out his office
a red hot poker was smoking by his side
he marched to the right hand net
and seared a wee fellas neck with it
the man wailed n cowered like a sick dog
as the gaffer hesitated about pressing it into his cheek

maybe you useless miners will listen to a coal fire poker eh
I will be sticking this in your eyes next
accidents happen when youse dont pay attention at all times
I am not responsible for that boys death
youse are
all of you lazy pricks
that big nosed bastard was a good worker
the best one I had on here
and if I hear another fucking word about his send off
I swear to God I will end the lot of youse
in the unlikely event of an accident that leads to death
you are getting papped over

thats what your contract states

theres no room on my ship for storing rotting dead bodies

no fucking room

youse hear me

no room

no room

got it

good

let that be the end of it

nobody is taking a rest unless I say so

I will brand youse all

thats twice that wee bastard has been slacking off

and hes cost me my best man

cant get a decent worker from the mining towns

I told them to get me sailors n fishermen

but no

and this is what happens

I have to be the bad guy n discipline a bunch of retards

lets prove me wrong

and fucking work like real men for once.

beast

hunger pressing so far down his throat
that even the chunks of jellied vomit
and wet snotters on the wall
were starting to look appetising
started swallowing bitten off nails from fingers
and chewing scabs
licked the condensation on the metal bed frame
anything to take away the pain
tried stuffing scales n tails of the fish the next morning
but it came back out in a grey froth seconds after
lashed across the kidneys for stealing waste products
and if he ever tried that again
a bedroom of stars for the night was guaranteed
he nodded and wept for forgiveness
a broken twisted creature that was once a man.

frozen fish

minutes
mere minutes
if the fish were left on the deck too long
they would get too hard to cut gut n can
blunt knives were no match for frozen scales n sharp bones
instead of holding back production
and sorting a decent system for the number of men left canning
the gaffer just screamed to work harder
harder
harder
then to hold off with the nets when too much went to waste
then back whipping the deck n screaming
smashing what glass remained
fish gasping their last breaths
men doing the same
he studied his fingers in the dying light
dented nails crusted with dirt n fish blood
skin scabbed scarred n bleeding
but all five still worked
he had that
most on board didnt.

falling to pieces

he warmed beside the engine room door
and thawed like a snowman in July
but even when his skin absorbed the warmth
he still felt cold
like his insides wouldnt unfreeze
a layer of bubbling ice
slush for blood
permafrost in lungs that couldnt be reached
even when skin pinked
and sweat broke
an ice creature of the dark that needed put out its misery
cold hands
cold head
cold heart
he rubbed his palms n watched the dust flake
skin was peeling off his face
feet
lips lathered with scabs
left before the wailing n night sweats arrived

staggered to his empty open coffin and tumbled inside
two days earlier
hed managed to get another blanket off an empty bed
the difference was like hot apple crumble
with an extra serving of custard
he curled into a ball n pain rinsed into his head
inspected an object by the light of the lamp
the top half of his left ear had folded off on to the pillow
skin around it crusted dark red n black
held the dismembered hunk of flesh between closed palms
and fell into sleeps wet arms.

– 103 –

expiring

you can feel it
feel it when you are dying
feel it like a pulse in your bones
along your skin
in flesh deep and shallow
pain rippling
organs calling out that something is wrong
extremely wrong
everything indicating its breaking down
to stop
sound the siren
and attempt to save what hasnt shut down n shrivelled
or death on a galloping horse will approach
the only certainty
but there wasnt a choice
he would be back out in the cold in a few hours
in blue wilderness
milking the last of his body dry.

- 104 -

and so it was

felt as weak as he ever had
lungs inflating with the feeling of dread
could feel sweat dripping from his armpits
thoughts sloshing from side to side
but dragged himself out of that bed
if he didnt they would be on him like flies
numbers dwindled still
the first catch of the day was dumped
twice the number that filled the net the day before
dying fish splashed n tried to swim out the puddles on deck
sleet lashed from the sky
the gaffer shouted his usual spiel then sank out the cold
his men dragged out the last of the latecomers
and headed behind him to his office
with cards and cigars on their breath
their laughter from that warm room
that was the crack that shattered the ice
one of the red headed brothers rose
scattered his cans n stared

arms trembling

the other mimicked his elders move

then launched an open can far into the sea

the mens ears pricked

a few followed suit

the rest froze like the prey animals they were

Jack stopped working

swallowed shards of broken glass

rose

booted over his cans

and nodded to the brothers in solidarity

dead if they did

dead if they didnt

the dark eyed fella rose n helped swollen hands to his feet

the netters let the nets sizzle n hit the sea

soon all work on deck had stopped

a cheer rose but faded in a few heartbeats

panic flooded

waiting for the inevitable response to come.

- 105 -

my wife

whats left of me without you
my sweet love
I never should have gone
all we had left was each other
and I left you
this ocean of blood
it changed me
who am I now
whats left of that man I once was
this new layer thats oiled itself over skin n bone
filled up the cracks and hardened
I have his memories buried in flaking skin
his pain
hurt
but Im not the same
the old me is being shedded
and dragged behind like a shadow of damp skin
I would scream if I had the energy
but Ill be home

I promise Ill be home
let the wind take my words to your ears
Ill get back to the man I was
back before we drifted on different currents
make things right between us
I belong with you
not here
always have
always will.

- 106 -

mutiny

a burnt smell in the air
the gaffer burst out the office seething with anger

youse have all lost a weeks wages
no in fact make that two weeks
and I will make it a fucking month if youse test me again
I mean it
dont fucking try me
pick up those cans n nets
and get back to work before youse lose any more
thats my final warning
go on

the first men held their stance
and nobody wavered
fists clenched
the murmur of voices swelled into a roar
the gaffer returned with a rifle
blew a hole in the nearest chest

and returned the swell to silence

youse will listen now eh
dont fuck with me
get back to work
or I will fucking shoot the lot of you
dont think for a second I wont

Jack gripped his gutting knife
as did the other canners
as blood n bits of wet flesh ran between their feet
the gaffer had only six men
one rifle
there were over twenty of them
I SAID GET BACK TO WORK

for the first time Jack saw fear twitching on that face
he fired again n again
but as if one startled creature the men rushed forward baring teeth
the gun was wrestled out his grip
guttural violence poured out throats n hands
the gaffers men were sliced n stabbed
and launched overboard with silent voices
the gaffer pleaded on soiled knees
said he would turn the ship around
and they would all be paid double
pink saliva dripped from lying lips
triple

pleaded n pleaded
even as his throat was cut n torn
he wriggled on the deck like a dying wasp in winter
careful to avoid the sting
old swollen hands sank a knife under his jaw
and extinguished the last breath
thirsty in death his chin bubbled like a stew
and all simmered to silence.

- 107 -

adrift

the survivors dragged the wailing cook out his den

plunged his head into a pot of rancid bile hed a cheek to call dinner

and tossed him and the soup overboard

emptied the kitchen

smeared hidden chocolate n sugar all over their faces

ransacked the gaffers office

singing

laughing

shouting

bottles n goodwill passed about like it was Hogmanay

new kings were crowned

and madness frothed on the still waters

Jack inched away

blood slept in black tongues on the floor with no man to bother it

he took a brush n swept it off the sides

and watched as it dripped into the pale below like treacle

stared into the blue void

eyes nipping

a nameless distance away was his home town

a memory of a dream it seemed so long ago
the cabin boy with soapy eyes appeared from hiding
asked if he was going to be killed
Jack said he didnt think so
he was only a wee boy
and he didnt do anything wrong
the boy nodded n smiled n wiped his wet face
but best to find an empty bunk
and keep to himself until things calmed down
there were a few beds in his room that were free
he would take him n get him some food to lay low with
there was a lot of madness on the ship
and it could flow in any direction.

- 108 -

the gathering storm

by nightfall the atmosphere changed again
a cloud of needles
raindrops cracked the surface of the calm water
now what
a ship full of canned sea meat
anybody who knew where it was going was dead
none of them getting a shilling for all that work
hung was more likely if they didnt have a believable story
whispers of who would be a grass
the mythical clipe was still to be found
more throats were cut
including old swollen hands
the cabin boy clawed out his new bed n tossed overboard
Jack was held down with a knife inching under his jaw
he managed to pull free as fingers pointed to another
more n more suspicions of potential traitors
hardly a sailor left alive amongst them
find a buyer in Aberdeen was the plan
split fourteen ways

thirteen ways

twelve

he hid in his bunk under a stained sheet

and sipped salty juice from a can

feeling panic rise n fall with every breath

but was found in the wee hours of the night

and dragged to the deck

breaths weakening

paper skull

the skin on his lips tore as he eased them open

the fuck he was a clipe

said they all needed to calm the fuck down

he didnt want an even cut

only enough to get back home

the red headed brothers kept him out of the firing line

said he was one of the first to start the mutiny

a bald islander had got his greasy hands on the stock whip and swung

but the eldest brother caught his arm

and chucked him n the whip screaming into the black water

the mood swayed to calm silence once more

and he was allowed to disappear back to the depths.

the architect

floating on the surface of the past

but soon that faded like chalk words in the rain

warped

couldnt hold a thought for more than a few seconds

fresh water dwindling

he stood on the deck where he used to work n stared out

the answers were there

the wind speaking to him n him alone

he smiled

the silence was so complete he heard nothing but sunshine

trees on the ocean appeared

smooth

as tall as houses

crashing up

revealing themselves from the foaming waves

branches bare

the ship moved through them like ghosts

he leaned over to touch

to feel one last time

nothing but water
he licked his wet hand n recoiled
the wind grabbed his thick spit before it left his tongue
it sailed out in a long salty thread around his cheek n neck
slumped
face pressed into the splintered boards
the architect of his own nightmare
waking impossible.

- 110 -

salt

the rainwater tank had been leaking since they departed
but with no maintenance men left it finally burst n emptied
taps dry
bottles nothing but fumes
men scooping out buckets from the sea
if they got deep enough
it was said to taste of the finest whisky known to man
he kept out of it
well out
incessant ringing in his remaining ear
balance all but gone
every single noise unbearable
he held onto the anchor n vomited
spat the acidic tang from his tongue
holding on with floating arms that pulsated with pins and needles
iron shoes
pints of saltwater being guzzled around him
washed what was left of the taste of home
of sanity

mouths full of oil

pushing away cups

not even an old fella having a seizure

and foaming at the mouth stopped the madness

the crunch of teeth cracking n crumbling in swollen gubs

men vomiting

and quenching their thirst with more salt

he lay flat on his back on deck

beams splitting at the seams underneath

and stared at the sky for some help to escape the watery void

any way out

but it was a language he couldnt read a word of.

unforgiving waters

a storm that was threatening to hatch for days
burst from above n below
the ship was ragdolled about the ocean
bunks crashed into walls
doors snapped and soared off into the night
masses n masses of the cans that drank their blood
were swept overboard
barrels boots nets n cages followed
the remaining porridge oats soaked in gallons of salt
by the time dawn arrived
and the waters calmed
there was hardly enough fish left to eat
never mind sell in Aber fucking deen
the ship was all but barren
a damp wind whistled through their soiled clothing
just head back was the consensus
Lerwick
Kirkwall
Peterhead

didnt matter what one
anywhere
just get to land n scatter
and forget they had ever boarded
he lay shivering in the engine room
seasoning the floor with sweat
palmed around in his own blood n vomit
hands trembling on the ends of dry withered stalks
fever swelling in marrow
anxiety burrowing
skin dissolving after being permanently soaked in saltwater.

- 112 -

fever dreams

men argued
coarse voices fading n rising
a long finger of nausea pressed into his stomach
turned as white as paper
eyes dreaming against the walls of the cabin
images of her spun n blurred to tears

I should never have went anywhere without you
I see that
when I get back we will pack
pack all our things
and say goodbye to that place
start again somewhere new
thats what you need
choose anywhere you want to go
anywhere
as long as I have you I dont need anything else
have you beside me once more
your warmth

your heartbeat
your love

her face twisted corkscrewed into his bellybutton
mashed long nails into his chest
his mouth was closed but he was screaming
screaming
screaming
screaming.

dark dream road

when Jack awoke
he was beside the engine
wrapped in three soiled blankets
eyes crisp n oozing with pockets of sleep
he drank a sip of water from a rusty bucket
a rush of nausea tipped his forehead
sweat broke out from his palms
and behind his knees
as dizziness folded his neck in half
he sat on the floor
and closed eyes to the spinning world
claws of angels around his wrists
passing out or vomiting were the only options
he danced his way back to the dark world
in a mixture of both.

- 114 -

recovery

the room was still
took a while to realise he was still on that death ship
folded away in its belly
silent eyes
whispering darkness
bruised skin had feeling once more
he rose from the floor
and wrapped a blanket around his shoulders
knives of light stabbed at his eyes
on deck was silent
eerie
the ship bobbed on the icy water
the sky was summer blue
and he could breathe through his nose again.

- 115 -

birthday

his seventh and final birthday
took the wee man to the Campsie hills
a roasting hot fifth of August
Erin had prepared a braw picnic spread
and even a wee sponge cake with candles
Jackie ran around playing in the stream
jumping n splashing
getting bit by a few water clegs didnt ruin a thing
Jack thought next year they would take him to the seaside
cos he hadnt seen it before
build sandcastles
collect shells
eat ice cream
but their boy never saw outside of their town after that
time congealed
cast into a grey domain
fear he couldnt rid them of.

- 116 -

engine

rags of snow on the water
any day now
they would be back home
any day now
the lie he told himself leaked out with the ulcers under his tongue
arguments boiled over if they were even going the right way
colours drained from the black stained walls n red faces
all was the colour n taste of ash
they all felt what was coming
but no one voiced their fate
silence
as though all noise was soaked up by a sponge
the metallic droning of the engine evaporated as daylight faded
men hammered n twisted metal into metal
but it was no use
oil had been leaking for countless miles
in a thin black river
the engine was flooded n fucked
as were they.

- 117 -

to be a man

I never got to see you grow up
you would have been the best of men
not one person didnt think you were the best wee boy
the best in the whole world
not one
even after the worst of days
your wee smile would melt it all away
I wish it was me that got sick
I should have been the one not you
not you
from the day you were born
all I wanted to do was protect you
give you the best life I could
take all of your worries
and leave you with none
as you made your way towards being a man
I failed
I failed you
I didnt know what to do

but if I had done things differently
even just something different
maybe you wouldnt have gotten sick
I wracked my brain for answers
to one conclusion
its my fault
it was my job to know
keep you safe
failed
I failed.

another storm a brew

the skies were dark grey n rumbling for days
the sea boiling thick with smog
few dared peek out from below

it will pass
will pass
just like the last one n the one before it
at the mercy of the water
Jack stood at the back of the ship beside the dark eyed fella
both throwing up chunks
hands coated in sticky saliva n bile
staring at the foaming white swells as they rose n rose
needed to get back inside
but limbs were chalk
the winds voice turned to a scream
waves a hundred times the size of a bing dump approached
Jack gasped as he was sprayed by molten horses
and they were washed across the deck
he reached out for anything

anything

anything

and finally found a handful of tangled netting

twisted a leg n arm to the pit

and hoped not to be ripped out to sea

wave after wave after wave after wave

all higher than any Glasgow tenement

the dark eyed fella was swept off the side screaming

Jack waited for a lull n slid to the stairs

just managed to get the door open

before another wave swung like a hammer

rushed back to his broken bunk

and held on with the little strength he had left

soaking

trembling

didnt feel any safer inside

wind dragged them in spirals

prayers being screamed out from lungs in an offkey chorus

he dug knuckles into red eye sockets n swallowed

hadnt been to the chapel in many a year

this shattering vessel their final hymn.

to the lighthouse

first light

the ship wasnt moving

the constant rocking motion had stopped some hours before

in darkness he palmed out from under his bunk

drenched in stale seawater n blood

they had landed on a wee rocky island

nests of dried mud long since abandoned

white rocks caked in bird shit

the survivors crawled out the sinking wreckage

pockets full of remaining tins

hoping against hope

an unlit lighthouse

a decrepit building hacked into the barren rock

seemed like the only shelter

the door unlocked

they poured in like molten lava

in a seat thick with dust sat a wilted corpse in an oversized jumper

no food to be found

a crate of cobwebbed brandy was burst out from a desk

and devoured

he undressed out his soaking clothing

and saw what he felt but dreaded to look at all morning

left arm snapped at the elbow

the red headed brothers tied it with rope

and the pain almost knocked him out

in a smoky room a fire breathed into life

voices hushed

and all were passed out n snoring within the hour.

- 120 -

wrong shore

to feel dirt under my feet again
to walk without the tilt n sway
is this what I wished for
this forsaken rock
maybe this is all I deserve
this refuge of grief n misery
escape the ship
but not the sea
wrapped up in the glen n the hills
in her arms
nevermore
famished waves waiting to feast
to drink the red within
only a matter of time
not if
but when.

- 121 -

foreign lands

days passed in broken whispers
buttery patches of drying blood on the floor
a half decayed seal carcass was found lying on the rocks
the men tore into it as if it was made of chocolate
the blubber was crawling with maggots
and those were eaten too
what remained of the ship was only useful for firewood
melting rubber belched a thick black smoke
consuming the island
deck boards hacked n burned to thick ash
heating swollen bones in shrinking skin
none of them had the foggiest idea where they were
a couple of torn maps and three coverless books
found in a drawer
all in a foreign language
the best guess it was Danish or Norwegian
all tossed in the fire n burnt to end the discussion
somewhere in the Arctic circle
wouldnt be long before there wasnt anything left to keep them
warm.

- 122 -

the netherworld

time melted through eyelids
and cold sweat dripped from his forehead
coughed n wiped the string from his chin
the air damp and foosty
the silent blue fed on their rock
nothing else around
in a new solid world
silence n darkness ascending from the deep
remains of the ship swept away by violent waves
as if it never existed
they lived like fish in a puddle
trying to set candles alight with water
men no longer men
time no longer time
all that was left was a song of the flies.

- 123 -

night

darkness clubbed the island across the jaw
all sleeping in one small room coated with sweet dripping nausea
huddled for warmth
arms folded n heads tucked into chests
in the one hour of grey solitary sunlight
from the side of the building
five of the nine remaining were prying out solid muck
and stuffing their faces
tasted like mince n tatties all mixed together one told Jack
better get stuck in while the going was good
the caked remains were spread around grey mouths
madness was stirring
a sound like blowing into an empty bottle
breaking n burning wood from tables n strips of the floor
sweat crawled down legs to ankles
shivering
talk of building a raft with the remaining wood and setting sail faded
as the first massive waves smashed into their thick glass tomb
nobody whispered any talk of being rescued
or even trying to fix the big light coated in scarfs of dust
this wasnt the land of the living any more
this was layers and layers under the darkest depths of hell.

- 124 -

the grave in the glen

had a dog when he was a wee boy called Kelly
an unwanted soul from a strays litter
loved that big bastard
gentle with all the street weans
ran around with him in the glen for hours on end
slept at the end of his bed
and was woken every morning with a big slabbery kiss
before anyone was up had fed Kelly
let him out for a pish in the garden
and they sat on the steps for the milkman n the wee postie
the farmer shot him while he was at school
ropes of blood swung from its neck
said Kelly bit one of his prize sheep
Jack cradled his dog in the cold muck
and buried him by his favourite tree in the glen
his father away in France
was powerless to do anything
his maw said best not to argue with important men
or there would be trouble

and they would be out on their ear
granny said it was an awful brute
and she was delighted to see the back of him
asked God
prayed all night for Kelly to come back to life
Rosary after Rosary
and they would run away together
but only silence replied
the grave in the glen remained untouched
never asked again.

chaos and panic

the two brass chamber pots were overflowing

and nobody would touch them

but the men still took to shitting in the sleeping room

using the corners n walls

too cold to go outside to empty anything

the violent scent burned

most of them sat in darkness

filthy in their rags

knees against marked chests

tongues swollen with thirst

gout puffin up ankles

the bed that once housed the lightkeeper was hacked to bits

sheets burned

walls splashed with spit n wailing

the stench rose

as did their laughter

Jack still went outside

and moved out to the main room

hanging onto what humanity was left with fingerless hands.

- 126 -

injury

in pale dawn
he went to the water
the air that pushed in from the ocean was so cold it burned like fire
took off his jumper to inspect his broken arm
the undergarment was stuck to the skin
thick lines of red n yellow pus ran as he pulled it free
a cry like a wild animal escaped his gub
he pressed the scab n more burst out
the elbow joint was swollen
double the size of the other
blackened flesh had spread
he lay on his front n dipped the arm into the searing sea
pain was good
it was good
the saltwater ate n washed
when he pressed again the wound was empty
covered it with that greasy wool jumper
and focused on anything but the coursing pulsing pain
the freezing cold a welcomed distraction.

seabird

a white seabird had circled the lighthouse all morning
landed in an insipid rock pool n ducked its head under
Jack hobbled outside n smiled
maybe there was other land not too far away
could see what direction it departed for
and work out a way of getting there
the men spilled out like cursed fiends n approached it
a friendly whistle drew the birds attention
the lisped man crept behind n grabbed it by the neck
it struggled as he ripped its head off n drank
the others flocked to him
and ate the creature raw
tearing feathers n its belly open
Jack went back inside
wanted to feel numb
was far from it.

- 128 -

the return

to stand in that glen once more
breathe the air drifting from the long green hills
and take a dauner through the trees to that wee house
open the door
and smell the purple heather she always had by the window
see her face again
to be home n walk those halls
climb those red flowered stairs
sleep in that bed
take me back
the way was closed
and no door on the lighthouse opened to it
maybe a scab in the wind would make it
the whole was like the rocks
at the mercy of the sea
to be worn down
and going nowhere anytime soon.

- 129 -

no saviours

pieces of smooth amber glass washed up in jagged rock pools
he put a piece in his mouth
and pressed it against the roof with a cut tongue
did little to ease off his thirst
puddles of rainwater were few and far between
and experiments with which ones werent salty
was a dangerous game to play on the edge
Jack sat by the shallows and looked for passing ships
but nothing but mist peered back from the distance
and the dark came once more
the dull scratch of silver water on the shore
nothing more existed
he stumbled back inside with the rest of the living dead
a swarm of pale sea beasts washed ashore from the deep
subhuman noises rising from each
crumbled into a ball on the floor
an abscess bubble ready to open behind teeth
and counted slowing breaths.

- 130 -

pieces of silver

what was this cruelty at the heart of men
all goodness gone for the pursuit of money
desperation
power
did it show the true side of all
the weak relying on mercy from the merciless
in a world where it had long been forgotten
prosperous times
but for who
someone always had to be sacrificed
always
that thirst for more never satisfied
he was one of the lambs
plenty more wool behind him
the slaughter never ending.

- 131 -

pink sky

black winged morning
dusty slabs of sunlight fell through the scars of rot in the roof
the new day came with a feeling of loss
the oldest fella
a kind factory worker with thick eyebrows
was splattered on the rocks
mutilated and clothes all stripped from bones
what was left of his face bobbing in the shallows
a grass was the whispering
the original grass
they had caught him
nobody admitting to doing him in
but in their collective delirium it was all making sense
finally got the real grass
could relax now the culprit had been found
Jack kept to himself
scouring the rocks for anything edible
sooking melted snow from that oily jumper
spilling like a cracked egg

seaweed as thick as a weans arm was stranded with them

slimy

brown black tentacles

stuck to hands if touched

he wandered in circles

pain gnawed from the cracks in his heels

and pooled in his sodden boots

threads like glass pierced their way into damp skin

shoulders hunching n twisting

lower back had a pulse of its own

mouth almost too swollen to swallow

his heart raced then slowed to almost nothing

then raced again

if he kept moving he was alive

death couldnt touch a moving man.

- 132 -

desire

a dark curl of smoke rose from the fireplace

joints pulsated against the wooden boards

pale as bone

sleep scratched a hole in his face

craving

craving for a pouch of baccy

just a wee draw of a cigarette

that would be the cure

would have clawed the eyes out of any man or woman

for just a wee taste

that was all that was needed

then he could think again

regain strength

and find a way home

just a wee taste was all that was needed

just a wee taste

he mouthed the request to the room

an empty bottle towards his head was the only reply.

- 133 -

coal

coal in the lighthouse long since used up
and none left in the bunker
at dawn he crawled into the main furnace
and covered his face n chest with the ashes
scrubbed his legs until skin bled
the smell of home caked into his hands once more
he scraped together a handful of dust
and poured it into his mouth
the taste of thousands of years under the ground
he was home
Erin n wee Jackie were waiting on the surface
waiting in their wee house in Timber Town
dinner was on the stove
the table set
waiting for him to finish work
to come back to them.

- 134 -

flakes of grey

the wind blew in the night
and sealed the lost souls in the lighthouse in its damp arms
dark days had come and gone
there once was a fire
but now there was only ashes
cold
soiled
dead
and no matter what happened
the impossible wasnt an option
he was fading
veered far off the yellow road to recovery
too long ago to find his way back
the song of the darkening blue
of bellies rumbling
breaths rasping
how fragile they all were
how delicate life was for even the strongest.

each day closer

drifted by the water in white morning silence
a sharp hunger picked at the inner flesh
clothes no longer fitting
belt needing yet another hole
jumper drowning him
black sponge flesh on his feet
snaking up ankles
fingers purple and numb
another tooth fell out with a prod from his tongue
the skin around his broken arm foaming more black pus
and leaked out through his jumper
warmth n heartbeats
soft flesh n bones
ash n blood floating on the frantic shore
a wave kissed his eyeball
he knelt on the rocks
and dipped his head into the icy water
to feel something
to feel he was still alive
was getting impossible to tell.

- 136 -

locked

the sky glowed milk red
and the water sparkled in the fading sunlight
the door to the lighthouse was boarded n locked
wind whipping at his back
he stood mute n motionless
took hours to be let back in
they had to be careful the men said
didnt know who was out there
the gaffer was out at sea
and he would be looking for them
had to make sure he wasnt a spy sent to gather evidence
he crawled to a dark grey fire
belching with smoke from burning boots
that melted to a puddle in the flames.

- 137 -

the miner

he awoke with all eyes fixated on him
jaw locked from the cold n clicked when he moved
a thick odour of bodies washed through the stale air
bones jutting out weather worn clothes
the lisped man crawled towards him
leaned over
and wrapped him in the teeth with jagged knuckles
had to header him to stop the rain of punches
both of them scurried away in opposite directions
like wounded animals
the lisped man spat red n screamed
they all just wanted to work on that ship n not kill anyone
but he figured it all out
the miner convinced them to murder
convinced them to kill the gaffer in cold blooded murder
convinced them to kill the gaffers men
innocent men who were just doing their jobs
the rest of them were all good men
but he was the beast

Satan himself

the red headed brothers helped Jack to his feet

and guided him away to a vacant corner

needed to be careful they said

stick with them

the others were out for more blood

been whispering all sorts of mental thinking

had made knives from the bed frame

and were sharpening them

nothing but miners left to hunt

the three sat backs to the glass

eyes to the remaining five

mottled blue grey flesh

mute as rocks

all shattered

white eyes in the dark that gave back the light

none of them taking the opiate of sleep

a stairway of saliva hung from the tallest brothers chin

empty faces

so young

twenty at most

yet suffering the fate of diseased old men

moonlight shining into darkness

leaving no scars on that wild n screaming sea behind them

felt tears running

the calling of the void

my son

my son.

- 138 -

laugh

I mind the first time I heard my wee boy laugh
I got home from work
nursing a heavy cold
head hanging off
arms n legs bruised n aching
the wee man was lying on the floor by the fire
looking at me
I smiled and made a face
and he let out this perfect wee giggle
I remember it well
as clear as if it just happened this morning
I lifted him up n danced about the room
I could have cried.

- 139 -

spiders

in predawn dark Jack heard the floor creak
from the glow from the fire
he saw the lisped man smiling like a carved turnip
and the netters frothing behind
all crawling towards them like sea spiders
knives in their dripping mouths
Jack shook the red headed brothers awake
you three are not welcome in here
miners digging their whole lives
digging to bring the darkness to the surface
and condemn us all
grasses grasses grasses grasses
we have to stop youse
before youse try to frame us innocents
we are innocent
fucking innocent
should have killed you all on the ship
I said to do it
I said it n said it n said it

I knew right away what youse were
I knew it
could taste the devil in your words
see it in your faces
wont make that mistake again
oh no
no no
from now on
I will always listen to the Lord when he speaks to me
and he said you are not welcome in here
told me to cast you back to the dark to be judged

a knife swung n opened one of the brothers cheeks
it flapped n ran thick with blood
Jack kicked out as they circled
his heart pumped against the thin bones in his chest
glanced at the door
and hoped it wasnt locked.

- 140 -

no escape

the room was as if in slow motion

each waiting for the other to flinch

starved beasts with the taste for blood

Jack readied to go for a face

the bleeding brother pulled off his belt

and swung over his shoulder

swung again n again

caught the biggest netter in the scarred space where his ear used to be

eyes widened

he swung a final time against the glass behind

and provided enough distraction to make their move

Jack felt a blade slice open the back of his thigh

he clenched his teeth n kept going

sprinting through the web of fire for the door

it opened with a single pull

and they leapt out into the freezing dark

panic frothed as they launched over wet rock

he peered back n the others had swarmed after

chased them down to the sea front

he slipped on the seaweed
and landed on his hip feeling it shatter
he fished out a rock from an icy pool
and launched it behind hearing a crack
launched another
and another
and another
screaming with every bit of breath
but nothing more than whispers floated out
a child like wailing from behind filled the air
then all went to silence
he pushed himself up n swung his head
the pursuers were gone
red headed brothers nowhere to be seen
he hobbled as far away from the lighthouse as possible
and curled under a ledge
blood leaked out from his nose
and crusted around nostrils in black knots
he picked the scab n took in a deep breath
the air smelled of rain but none to be seen
boots were soaking
limbs twitching
uncontrollable shivering
flickering stars infested his vision
daylight no refuge.

last goodbye

my dearest wife
how I long to be beside you
hold you to my chest
and tell you everything will be all right
that we will get through it together
and come out the other side
I now know I cant
Im so sorry
forgive me
please forgive me
if I could only come back today
I would never let you down again
in those last months
I should have kissed you more
held you more
told you I loved you more
breaks my heart I never will again
but Ill meet you on the other side of these black waters
hold you both again

and never let go

in this world

all is lost

gone

let me live in dreams

of you

of us.

- 142 -

to die

a sea of clouds devoured the last of the early evening light
mutilated twilights
snow falling in big wet flakes
ashes of clothes on his damp body
he stood staring into the foaming white water
trembling
ruptured before a frozen sea god
silent
in silence
nowhere left to hide in his wet paper skin
wine coloured muck in his fingernails
starved men at his back
knew he was the real grass they hissed
oh they knew for certain
he was the gaffers special boy all along
he had cut the nets so they couldnt catch anything
sent them out to the deeper waters instead of home
dumped all the cans overboard with those ginger traitors
made them crash

he made them fucking crash into this prison
the red headed brothers were lying chests to the rocks
filling shallows
limbs n cartilage ripped n scattered from frenzied morning attacks
moth like hands reached out
Jack turned and saw eyes bulging
grey crust wrapped over white bones
stained red teeth n gums
he made a fist with his unbroken arm
but there wasnt enough strength to swing
knees buckled
defeat fell over him like a fine dust
he didnt feel the first rusty blade into his shoulder
but the second into his liver twisted pain long since buried
cried out
fell to his knees as rocks caved in his skull
the white world paled
paled
and closed around with withered arms.

Love Your Book

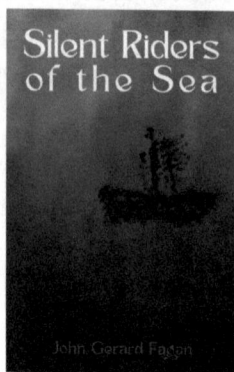

Silent Riders of the Sea

TIMELINE

NOVEMBER 2024

Soft-back book printed from paper that has been carbon offset through the World Land Trust Scheme.

PRINTED by Hobbs the Printers Ltd
at Southampton, United Kingdom

PUBLISHED by Cybirdy Publishing
London, United Kingdom

CYBIRDY
Publishing Limited

SPECIAL EDITION
Autographed by the Author

John Gerard Fagan

WHO are you?	WHO did you obtain the book from?	WHEN did you obtain the book
FIRST GUARDIAN		
SECOND GUARDIAN		
THIRD GUARDIAN		
FOURTH GUARDIAN		
FIFTH GUARDIAN		

John Gerard Fagan is a Scottish writer from Muirhead in the outskirts of Glasgow, who currently lives in Dunbar. His memoir *Fish Town*, about buying a one-way ticket to rural Japan, where he lived for seven years, was published in 2021. *Silent Riders of the Sea* is his first work of long fiction.